Woman Talk

Volume Two

Also by Michèle Brown
and Ann O'Connor

WOMAN TALK: A Woman's Book of Quotes, Volume One
which covers:
Women on Women
The Inner Woman – Health and Nourishment
The Outer Woman – Beauty and Fashion
Men
Love
Sex
Marriage
Children
Life
Society
Friendship and Loneliness
Religion
Work
Success and Failure

Woman Talk

Volume Two

A Woman's Book of Quotes

Michèle Brown
&
Ann O'Connor

Macdonald

To our daughters

A Macdonald Book

First published in Great Britain in 1985
by Macdonald & Co (Publishers) Ltd
London & Sydney

British Library Cataloguing in Publication Data

Woman talk.
2 : A woman's book of quotes
1. Women—Quotations, maxims, etc.
I. Brown, Michele II. O'Connor, Ann
305.4 PN6084.W6

ISBN 0-356-10628-4

Typeset, printed and bound in Great Britain by
Hazell Watson & Viney Limited
Member of the BPCC Group
Aylesbury, Bucks

Macdonald & Co (Publishers) Ltd
Maxwell House
74 Worship Street
London EC2A 2EN
A BPCC plc Company

ACKNOWLEDGEMENTS

In compiling the two volumes of this collection of quotations we have used material gathered from a vast variety of sources, ranging from newspaper articles, chance remarks heard on TV and elsewhere, magazine features, biographies. Among the books we have consulted are:

A Solitary Woman, Henrietta Sharpe (Constable); *The Memoirs of Sarah Bernhardt*, Ed. Sandy Lesberg (Peebles Press); *Just Barbara*, Barbara Woodhouse (Michael Joseph and Rainbird); *Amy Johnson*, Constance Babington Smith (White Lion); *Audacity to Believe*, Sheila Cassidy (Collins); *Virginia Woolf and Her World*, John Lehmann (Thames & Hudson); *Lilian Baylis: The Lady of the Old Vic*, Richard Findlater (Allen Lane); *Horatia Nelson*, Winifred Gerin (Oxford University Press); *Marie Stopes: A Biography*, Ruth Hall (André Deutsch); *Eminent Victorians*, Lytton Strachey (Chatto); *The Pelican Guide to English Literature* (Penguin); *The Talkies*, Richard Griffith (Dover Press); *Ellen Wilkinson*, Betty D. Vernon (Croom Helm); *Chanel*, Edmonde Charles-Roux (Jonathan Cape); *On Lies, Secrets and Silence*, Adrienne Rich (Virago); *The Female Eunuch*, Germaine Greer (Paladin); *Graffiti*, Nigel Rees (Unwin); *Miss Piggy's Guide to Life*, Muppet Press (Michael Joseph); *My Favourite Comedies in Music*, Victor Borge & Robert Sherman (Robson Books); *Off the Wall*, Rachel Bartlett (Proteus); *Now for the Good News*, Robert Dougall (Mowbrays); *Dylan Thomas*, Andrew Sinclair (Michael Joseph) *The Encyclopaedia of Insulting Behaviour* (Futura); *Beecham Stories*, Ed. Harold Atkins & Archie Newman (Robson Books); *The Bandsman's Daughter*, Irene Thomas (Macmillan); *Violets and Vinegar*, Jilly Cooper & Tom Hartman (Allen & Unwin); *The Complete Husband*, Gyles Brandreth (Sidgwick and Jackson); *Woman, Fancy or Free*, Nan Berger & Joan Maizels (Mills and Boon); *A Summer Bird-Cage*, Margaret Drabble (Weidenfeld & Nicolson); *Side Effects*,

Woody Allen (New English Library); *My Cousin Beatrix*, Ulla Hyde Parker.

Thanks to one and all.

APOLOGY

It has been our wish to give brief background information concerning the authors of all quotations used; sometimes, however, our efforts have been unsuccessful. We therefore extend our apologies to those whose words are attributed by name only.

CONTENTS

INTRODUCTION

Despite the many advances towards equality made by women in the last 150 years we still have a long way to go before their abilities are accepted without remark, excuse or explanation. In 1763 Dr Johnson was quoted by Boswell as saying, 'Sir, a woman's preaching is like a dog's walking on his hinder legs. It is not done well; but you are surprised to find it done at all.' In 1984 a jumbo jet was piloted across the Atlantic by a woman for the first time. This was covered by the newspapers as something of an event, although presumably no more brute force is required to pilot a jumbo than to fly any other passenger plane. There may be some value to reporting these individual achievements if only to encourage others to compete and succeed in the most demanding and stimulating careers open to men and women in the twentieth century. However, the spirit of Dr Johnson was seen still to stalk openly throughout the land, for the main burden of the newspaper report was that 'womanlike' the pilot emerged breathless and wide-eyed having viewed the sunrise as she flew towards Europe. In a world which still finds cause for comment when women work and achieve on equal terms with men, and which needs simultaneously to reassure itself that they have not lost their 'feminine' qualities in doing so (implying equally fatuously that men lack those same qualities); where serious discussions still take place as to whether or not women news readers destroy the credibility of what they are reporting (despite the fact that many of the main news makers are women) it is not surprising that women still feel the need to group together to emphasize their talents and abilities. In the first volume of *Woman Talk* former Wimbledon champion Virginia Wade is quoted saying, 'Winners aren't popular. Losers usually are.' No one wants to be unpopular yet a quick dip into the section headed Sexism will give a flavour of the great unpopularity of achieving women in the eyes of many men. As a result we still feel the need to group together, publishing anthologies of women's verse, women's plays and women's novels. When there are no longer publishing houses specializing in women writers and pages in newspapers devoted to 'women's subjects' then there will no longer be a necessity for a collection of 'women's' quotes. Until that happy day we make no apology for publishing this second volume of *Woman Talk*. While we were preparing the first volume we soon realized that there was far too much material for one book and we are grateful to the publishers for allowing us a second volume rather than forcing us to make impossible choices about what should stay and what should go. Any collection of women's quotations would have been incomplete without such famous lines as Dorothy Parker's remark as a second-rate starlet left a restaurant where she was dining, 'There goes the good time that's been had by all', but two volumes have given us the chance to widen our scope and include quotations which are less well known. This second volume has also allowed us to give men a chance to redress the balance with a section entitled Men on Women. Best of all it has given us an opportunity to show the wide range of wit, wisdom and insight displayed by women of all ages and backgrounds. Whether or not you agree with everything they say we hope you will enjoy dipping into this fascinating collection as much as we have enjoyed compiling it.

Michèle Brown
Ann O'Connor

IN THE PUBLIC EYE

FRANKLYN PIERCE ADAMS
American writer
On US actress, Helen Hayes

She appears to be suffering from fallen archness.

PRINCE ALBERT (1819–1861)
Consort to Queen Victoria
On himself in a letter, 10 February 1840

In less than three hours I shall stand before the altar with my dear bride . . . God help me!

TSARINA ALEKSANDRA (1872–1918)
In a letter to the Tsar
In Leon Trotsky's *History of the Russian Revolution*, Vol. I

They accuse Rasputin of kissing women, etc. Read the Apostles; they kissed everybody as a form of greeting.

QUEEN ALEXANDRA (1844–1925)
Consort to King Edward VII
To Sir William Knollys, 11 October 1867
In Philip Magnus' *King Edward the Seventh*

I may be pale, but it is from anger at being obliged to see the King of Prussia, and not from cold.

PRINCESS ANNE (*b.* 1950)

There are always people around waiting for me to put my foot in it, just like my father.

When I appear in public people expect me to neigh, grind my teeth, paw the ground and swish my tail – none of which is easy.

On Captain Mark Phillips

He kept telling me he was a confirmed bachelor and I thought at least one knows where one stands.

A few days before her engagement to Captain Mark Phillips

There is no romance between us. He is here solely to exercise the horses.

ANONYMOUS

1936
Hark! the herald angels sing
Mrs Simpson pinched our king.

If Hitler were alive today the German girls wouldn't let him bomb London if the Beatles were there.

On Bette Davis

Nobody's as good as Bette when she's bad.

DR JOHN ARBUTHNOT (1667–1735)
In a letter to Jonathan Swift, 12 August 1713
On Queen Anne

I believe sleep was never more welcome to a weary traveller than death was to her.

WALTER BAGEHOT (1826–1877)
British economist and journalist
In *The English Constitution*
On Queen Anne

. . . one of the smallest people ever set in a great place.

On English writer Lady Mary Wortley Montagu (1689–1762)

Lady Mary lived before the age in which people waste half their lives in washing the whole of their persons.

TALLULAH BANKHEAD (1902–1968)
American film star

I'm as pure as the driven slush.

They used to photograph Shirley Temple through gauze. They should photograph me through linoleum.

JOHN BARRYMORE (1882–1942)
American actor

After the making of *Bill of Divorcement* Katharine Hepburn said to her leading man, John Barrymore, 'Thank God I don't have to act with you any more!'
'Oh,' replied Barrymore, 'I didn't know you ever had.'

SHIRLEY BASSEY
Welsh-born singer

I'd prefer to be known as the female Elvis Presley – he's the greatest showman since Liberace.

CECIL BEATON (1904–1980)
British photographer and designer
On Katherine Hepburn

She has a face that belongs to the sea and the wind, with large rocking-horse nostrils and teeth that you just know bite an apple every day.

RUDOLF BING (*b.* 1920)
American opera director
On Italian soprano, Renata Tebaldi

Very sweet and very firm . . . she has dimples of iron.

We finally accepted the fact that Beverly Sills of the City Opera, having been born in Brooklyn, was entitled to priority in the portrayal of British royalty.

MAX BEERBOHM (1872–1956)
British writer and caricaturist
On Queen Caroline, consort of George IV

Fate wrote her a most tremendous tragedy, and she played it in tights.

In *Saturday Review*, 30 August 1952

On novelist Marie Corelli

Her definition of a pessimist was – anyone who didn't like her unduly!

DAVID BEN-GURION (1886–1973)
Israeli statesman
On Golda Meir

The only man in my Cabinet.

BLACKWELL
American designer

Elizabeth Taylor looks like two small boys fighting underneath a mink blanket.

ANNE BOLEYN (1507–1536)
Second wife of Henry VIII
In her last letter to her husband by whose order she was later executed.

You have chosen me from a low estate to be your queen and companion, far beyond my desert or desire.

JOHN MASON BROWN (1900–1969)
American essayist and critic

Tallulah Bankhead barged down the Nile last night as Cleopatra, and sank.

DAME IVY COMPTON-BURNETT (1884–1969)
British writer
On herself, when asked about her life

There's not much to say. I haven't been at all deedy.

In a letter to Anthony Powell
On Emily Brontë

Posterity has paid its debt to her too generously, and with too little understanding.

LORD BYRON (1788–1824)
British poet
On his wife, Annabella Milbanke

The Princess of Parallelograms.

In Lady Blessington's *Conversations with Lord Byron*

Mrs Shelley is very clever, indeed it would be difficult for her not to be so; the daughter of Mary Wollstonecraft and Godwin, and the wife of Shelley, could be no common person.

LADY BYRON (Annabella Milbanke) (1792–1860)
On Lord Byron

In his endeavours to corrupt my mind he has sought to make me smile first at Vice, saying 'There is nothing to which a woman may not be reconciled by repetition or familiarity'. There is *no* Vice with which he has not endeavoured in this manner to familiarize me.

HAROLD CACCIA
In Harold Macmillan's *Riding the Storm*, 1971
On the happy effect of Elizabeth II's visit to the United States

She had buried George III for good and all.

MARIA CALLAS (1923–1977)
Opera singer

First I lost my weight, then I lost my voice, and now I lost Onassis.

I know I have a reputation for bad manners, but I am always having good tempers.

MRS PATRICK CAMPBELL (1865–1940)
British actress
On Tallulah Bankhead

Watching Tallulah on stage is like watching somebody skating on thin ice. Everyone wants to be there when it breaks.

QUEEN CAROLINE (1768–1821)
Wife of George IV
Jingle during her divorce trial, 1820

Most Gracious Queen, we thee implore
To go away and sin no more

But if that effort be too great,
To go away at any rate.

MAMA CASS (Elliott) (1943–1974)
American rock singer

I don't have the psychology of the fat girl. I don't hide in corners. I'm a very verbose person.

CATHERINE OF ARAGON (1485–1536)
First wife of Henry VIII

I have done England little good, but I should be sorry to do it any harm.

SIR HENRY (Chips) CHANNON (1897–1958)
American-born diarist
On Queen Mary, consort to George V

Queen Mary looking like the Jungfrau, white and sparkling in the sun.

CHER (*b.* 1946)
American singer

Maybe I'm not talented. Maybe I'm just the Dinah Shore of the 'sixties. The square people think I'm too hip and the hip people think I'm too square. And nobody likes my choice of men – everybody thinks I'm fucking the Mormon Tabernacle Choir.

SARAH CHURCHILL (1660–1744)
Duchess of Marlborough

On Queen Anne
(She) had a person and appearance not at all ungraceful, till she grew exceeding gross and corpulent.

. . . Her friendships were flames of extravagant passion ending in aversion.

I fancy that anybody that had been shut up so many tedious hours as I have been, with a person that had no conversation, and yet must be treated with respect, would feel something of what I did, and be very glad, when their circumstances did not want it, to be freed from such a slavery.

WINSTON CHURCHILL (1874–1965)
British statesman
In *History of the English-Speaking Peoples*
On Queen Boadicea

The citizens of London implored Suetonius to protect them, but when he heard that Boadicea, having chased Cerialis towards Lincoln, had turned and was marching south, he took the hard but right decision to leave them to their fate.

On Lady Astor

She reigns on both sides of the Atlantic in the Old World and the New, at once as a leader of fashionable society, and of advanced feminist democracy. . . . She denounces the vice of gambling in unmeasured terms, and is closely associated with an almost unrivalled racing stable. She accepts Communist hospitality and flattery, and remains the Conservative Member for Plymouth.

'If you were my husband I'd poison your coffee,' Lady Astor told Sir Winston during one of their many confrontations. 'If you were my wife, I'd drink it,' he replied.

JEAN COCTEAU (1889–1963)
French poet and playwright
To Marlene Dietrich

Your name begins with a caress and ends with the crack of a whip.

On Marlene Dietrich

A frigate, a figurehead, a Chinese fish, a lyrebird, a legend and a wonder.

COLUMBIA PICTURES
Studio comment on Marilyn Monroe

Can't act . . . Voice like a tight squeak . . . Utterly unsure of herself . . . Unable even to take refuge in her own insignificance.

ALISTAIR COOKE (*b.* 1908)
British-born journalist
On Greta Garbo

When you start to write about (her), you are reminded more forcibly than ever that practically all the criticism of emotional acting we have reads like a fourth-form essay on the character of Napoleon.

DONALD COOK (1900–1961)
American actor
On Tallulah Bankhead

With Tallulah, a leading man has an exhausting time offstage.

GEORGE CUKOR (*b.* 1899)
American film director
In Gavin Lambert's *On Cukor*
On Marilyn Monroe

If she was a victim of any kind, she was a victim of friends.

On Jean Harlow

Jean Harlow was very soft about her toughness.

BETTE DAVIS (*b.* 1908)
American actress

There's only one of us in each country.

In *The Lonely Life*
On Rudolf Valentino

(He) had silently acted out the fantasies of women . . . (he) and his world were a dream. A whole generation of females wanted to ride off into a sandy paradise with him. At thirteen I had been such a female.

HOWARD DIETZ (*b.* 1896)
American writer
On Tallulah Bankhead

A day away from (her) is like a month in the country.

COLONEL DISBROWE
Chamberlain to Queen Charlotte, consort of George III
Yes, I do think that the *bloom* of her ugliness is going off.

BENJAMIN DISRAELI (1804–1881)
British statesman
To Queen Victoria, who had written *Leaves from the Journal in the Highlands*, 1868
We authors, Ma'am.

MRS DYKSTRA
On Thomas E. Dewey, American politician
He is just about the nastiest little man I've ever known. He struts sitting down.

ALBERT EINSTEIN (1879–1955)
German-born physicist
In Eve Curie's *Madame Curie*
Marie Curie is, of all celebrated beings, the only one whom fame has not corrupted.

QUEEN ELIZABETH I (1533–1603)
Speech to Parliament, 1586
As for me, I see no such great cause why I should either be fond to live or fear to die. I have had good experience of this world, and I know what it is to be a subject and what to be a sovereign. Good neighbours I have had, and I have met with bad: and in trust I have found treason.

To her soldiers at the approach of the Spanish Armada, 29 July 1588
I know I have but the body of a weak and feeble woman, but I have the heart and stomach of a king, and of a king of England too, and think foul scorn that Parma or Spain or any Prince in Europe should dare to invade the borders of my realm.

Speech to her first Parliament, 1559
And to me it shall be a full satisfaction both for the

memorial of my name, and for my glory also, if when I shall let my last breath, it be ingraven upon my Marble Tombe, *Here lyeth ELIZABETH* which raigned a Virgin, and dyed a Virgin.

In James Melville's *Memoirs*, 1683

The Queen of Scots is this day lighter of a fair son, and I am but a barren stock.

To Sir Walter Raleigh on his introduction of tobacco into England

I have known many persons who turned their gold into smoke, but you are the first to turn smoke into gold.

To her courtiers

Had I been crested, not cloven, my Lords, you had not treated me thus.

To the Bishop of Ely

Proud Prelate: You know what you were before I made you what you are now. If you do not immediately comply with my request, I will unfrock you, by God.

Contemporary folk poem on her death

She ruled this nation by herself
And was beholden to no man
She bore the sway of all affairs,
And yet was but a woman.

QUEEN ELIZABETH II (*b.* 1926)

On her twenty-fifth wedding anniversary

I think everybody really will concede that on this, of all days, I should begin my speech with the words 'My husband and I'.

I cannot forget that I was crowned Queen of the United Kingdom of Great Britain and Northern Ireland.

On Princess Margaret's children

They are not royal. They just happen to have me as their aunt.

QUEEN ELIZABETH THE QUEEN MOTHER (*b.* 1900)
In 1940
I'm glad we've been bombed. It makes me feel I can look the East End in the face.

On the National Anthem being played at the televised Cup Final
Oh, do turn it off, it's so embarrassing unless one is there – like hearing the Lord's Prayer when playing canasta.

My favourite programme is *Mrs Dale's Diary*. I try never to miss it because it is the only way of knowing what goes on in a middle-class family.

Things change so terribly fast these days. Look at the Shah of Iran, poor man.

DALE EVANS (*b.* 1912)
American actress
On her husband, screen cowboy Roy Rogers
In horse vernacular, Roy has always 'given me my head' and I have tried to do the same for him.

JOHN EVELYN (1620–1706)
English diarist
On Catherine of Braganza, consort to Charles II
The Queen arrived with a traine of Portugueze Ladys in their monstrous fardingals or *Guard-Infantas*: their complexions olivaster, & sufficiently unagreeable. . . .

CLIFTON FADIMAN (*b.* 1904)
American essayist
Gertrude Stein is the mama of Dada.

MARIANNE FAITHFULL (*b.* 1947)
British actress and rock singer
A symbol of the scarlet woman, that was my claim to fame.

FARAH (*b.* 1938)
Consort to the late Shah of Iran

I never forget that, as a woman, my position is a delicate one. In my country I am considered, whether I like it or not, the representative of feminine emancipation. Already these women, formerly regarded as chattels, without the right to be heard, have increasingly more to say for themselves.

FREDERICK THE GREAT (1712–1786)
On Austrian Arch-duchess Maria Theresa's part in the partition of Poland

She is always in tears at 'poor Poland' yet she is always ready to take her share.

THOMAS FULLER (1608–1661)
On Jane Seymour (1509–1537), consort to Henry VIII. She died giving birth to his only son.

Of all the wives of King Henry she only had the happiness to die in his full favour, the 14th of Octob. 1537 and is buried in the quire of Windsor Chappell, the King continuing in real mourning for her even all the Festival of Christmas.

ZSA ZSA GABOR (*b.* 1919)
Hungarian-born actress

I never hated a man enough to give him his diamonds back.

GRETA GARBO (*b.* 1905)
Swedish actress

I never said 'I want to be alone'. I only said 'I want to be let alone'.

GEORGE IV (1762–1830)

When Prince of Wales, October 1811

On a political marriage for him despite his private marriage to Mrs Fitzherbert.

Damn the North! and damn the South! and damn

Wellington! the question is, how am I going to get rid of this damned Princess of Wales?

BRENDAN GILL
In *New Yorker*, 7 October 1972
On Tallulah Bankhead

She learned how little it takes to make people bleed, and sometimes she could not resist demonstrating her skill at this unpleasing game.

NELL GWYN (1651–1687)
English mistress of Charles II
To a hostile crowd which mistook her for the Catholic Duchess of Portland

Pray, good people, be civil, *I* am the Protestant whore.

GILBERT HARDING (1907–1960)
British broadcaster

When asked by Mae West's manager, 'Can't you sound a bit more sexy when you interview her?'

'If, sir, I possessed the power of conveying unlimited sexual attraction through the potency of my voice, I would not be reduced to accepting a miserable pittance from the BBC for interviewing a faded female in a damp basement.'

SIR JOHN HARRINGTON (1561–1612)
English writer and courtier
On Queen Elizabeth I

When she smiled it was pure sunshine, that everyone did choose to bask in, if they could: but anon came a storm from a sudden gathering of clouds, and the thunder fell in wondrous manner on all alike.

CHRISTOPHER HASSALL (1912–1963)
British writer
On Dame Edith Sitwell

She's genuinely bogus.

LILLIAN HELLMAN (1907–1984)
American playwright

It is a mark of many famous people that they cannot part with their brightest hour.

KATHARINE HEPBURN (*b.* 1909)
On Fred Astaire and Ginger Rogers

He gives her class and she gives him sex.

LORD HERVEY (1696–1743)
On Caroline of Ansbach, consort to George II

She was with regard to power as some men are to their amours, the vanity of being thought to possess what she desired was equal to the pleasure of the possession itself.

LEIGH HUNT (1784–1859)
British writer and poet
On actress, Sarah Siddons

She can overpower, astonish, afflict, but she cannot win; her majestic presence and commanding features seem to disregard love, as a trifle to which they cannot descend.

CLIVE JAMES (*b.* 1939)
Australian critic
On Marilyn Monroe

She was good at playing abstract confusion in the same way that a midget is good at being short.

NUNNALLY JOHNSON (*b.* 1897)
Hollywood film producer and screenwriter
On Marilyn Monroe

A phenomenon of nature, like Niagara Falls and the Grand Canyon.

DR SAMUEL JOHNSON (1709–1784)
British writer
On Mary Wortley Montagu 20 March 1781 (quoted by James Boswell)

Mrs Montagu has dropped me. Now, Sir, there are people whom one should like very well to drop, but would not wish to be dropped by.

PAULINE KAEL (*b.* 1919)
American critic
On Robert Redford
In *Reeling*, 1976

He has turned almost alarmingly blond – he's gone past platinum, he must be plutonium; his hair is coordinated with his teeth.

FRED KEATING
On Tallulah Bankhead

I've just spent an hour talking to Tallulah for a few minutes.

EMERY KELEN
American journalist

Viscount Waldorf Astor owned Britain's two most influential newspapers, *The Times* and the *Observer*, but his American wife, Nancy, had a wider circulation than both papers put together.

DAME MARGARET (Madge) KENDAL (1849–1935)
British actress
On Sarah Bernhardt, who had a leg amputated

A great actress, from the waist down.

JOHN F. KENNEDY (1917–1963)
35th President of the United States
2 June 1961

I am the man who accompanied Jacqueline Kennedy to Paris and I have enjoyed it.

JOSEPH P. KENNEDY (1888–1960)
American ambassador to the UK
On Eleanor Roosevelt, wife of President Roosevelt

She bothered us more on our jobs in Washington to take care of the poor little nobodies than all of the rest of the people down there put together. She was always sending me a note to have some little Susie Glotz to tea at the Embassy.

SYLVIE KESHET
Quoted in *Time*, 6 July 1970
On Golda Meir

A dragon who pretends to be St George.

HENRY KISSINGER (*b.* 1923)
American statesman
On Eleanor Roosevelt

A symbol of compassion in a world of increasing righteousness.

On Indira Gandi

The lady is cold-blooded and tough and will not turn into a Soviet satellite merely because of pique.

JOHN KNOX (*c.* 1513–1572)
Scottish reformer
On Queen Mary I ('Bloody Mary')

Cursed Jezebel of England!

LADY CAROLINE LAMB (1785–1828)
English mistress of Lord Byron
In her *Journal*
On meeting Lord Byron, 1812

Mad, bad, and dangerous to know.

LILLIE LANGTRY (1853–1929)
British actress and mistress of Edward VII

I got on famously with Prince Edward until I put that piece of ice down his neck.

GERTRUDE LAWRENCE (1898–1952)
British-born musical comedy star

I am not what you'd call wonderfully talented but I am light on my feet and I do make the best of things. All I really lack is a private life.

OSCAR LEVANT (1906–1972)
American pianist
On Zsa Zsa Gabor

She not only worships the Golden Calf, she barbecues it for lunch.

ABRAHAM LINCOLN (1809–1865)
16th President of the United States
On Harriet Beecher Stowe, author of *Uncle Tom's Cabin*

So this is the little lady who made this big war. (*The American Civil War over the abolition of slavery*).

CLARE BOOTHE LUCE (*b.* 1903)
American writer and diplomat
On Eleanor Roosevelt

No woman has ever so comforted the distressed – or so distressed the comfortable.

LORETTA LYNN
American country and western singer
On Jimmy Carter

It's sure nice to have a President who don't speak with an accent.

THOMAS B. MACAULAY (1800–1859)
British historian
On Sarah, Duchess of Marlborough

She hated easily; she hated heartily; and she hated implacably.

On Queen Anne

Nature had made her a bigot. . . . It was a great thing to be the only member of the Royal Family who regarded Papist and Presbyterian with impartial aversion.

Anne… when in good humour, was meekly stupid, and when in bad humour, was sulkily stupid.

On Queen Mary II (1662–1694), consort to William III

Her understanding, though very imperfectly cultivated, was quick. There was no want of feminine wit and shrewdness in her conversation, and her letters were so well expressed that they deserved to be well spelt.

MARIE, QUEEN OF ROMANIA (1875–1938)
On Royalty

Like clowns, they amuse the people, even with their funerals, and keep them contented.

MARIA THERESA (1717–1780)
Archduchess of Austria
In a letter to her son

You ask my opinion about taking the young Saltzburg musician into your service. I do not know where you can place him, since I feel that you do not require a composer, or other useless people. . . . It gives one's service a bad name when such types run about the beggars; besides, he has a large family.

GROUCHO MARX (1895–1977)
American actor
In Marilyn Monroe's *My Story*

It's Mae West, Theda Bara, and Bo Peep all rolled into one.

MARY, QUEEN OF SCOTS (1542–1587)
On James Hepburn, Earl of Bothwell

I could follow him around the world in my nightie.

LOUIS B. MAYER (1885–1957)
Hollywood film producer
Message to Greta Garbo, via her agent

Tell her that in America men don't like fat women.

DAME NELLIE MELBA (1861–1931)
Australian opera singer

Never fall in love with royalty, they'll break your heart.

RALPH MCGILL
On Eleanor Roosevelt

One of the shameful chapters of this country was how many of the comfortable – especially those who profited from the misery of others – abused her. . . . But she got even in a way that was almost cruel. She forgave them.

MARSHALL MCLUHAN (1911–1980)
American social scientist
In *Understanding Media*
On Florence Nightingale

She began to think, as well as to live, her time, and she discovered the new formula for the electronic age: Medicare.

GEORGE MEREDITH (1828–1913)
British poet

George Eliot had the heart of Sappho; but the face, with the long proboscis, the protruding teeth of the Apocalyptic horse, betrayed animality.

BETTE MIDLER (*b.* 1945)
American entertainer

I too slept with Jack Kennedy.

I wouldn't say I invented tack, but I definitely brought it to its present high popularity.

MARY RUSSELL MITFORD (1787–1855)
British novelist
In a letter to Sir William Elford, 3 April 1815

I have discovered that our great favourite, Miss Austen, is my countrywoman . . . Mamma says that she was then the prettiest, silliest, most affected, husband-hunting butterfly she ever remembers.

GEORGE JEAN NATHAN (1882–1958)
American critic
On seeing the picture of Mae West as the Statue of Liberty

She looks more like the Statue of Libido.

On Eleanora Duse

She acted from the head down, not from the feet up. Her body was eloquent because her legs had less to do with manipulating it and guiding it than her brain.

EDNA O'BRIEN (*b.* 1936)
Irish writer

I'm a tuning fork, tense and twanging all the time.

JACQUELINE KENNEDY ONASSIS (*b.* 1929)
Former wife of the 35th President of the United States

I always wanted to be some kind of writer or newspaper reporter. But after college . . . I did other things.

DOROTHY PARKER (1893–1967)
American writer and wit
On Harold Ross, editor of *The New Yorker*

His improbabilities started with his looks. His long body seemed to be only basted together, his hair was quills upon the fretful porcupine, his teeth were Stonehenge, his clothes looked as if they had been brought up by somebody else.

BLAISE PASCAL (1623–1662)
French physicist

If Cleopatra's nose had been shorter, the whole face of the earth would have been changed.

SAMUEL PEPYS (1633–1703)
British diarist
On Nell Gwyn

Pretty, witty Nell.

S. J. PERELMAN (1904–1970)
American writer
On Theda Bara

. . . a pyrogenic half pint . . . who immortalized the vamp just as Little Egypt, the World's Fair of 1893, had the hoochie-coochie.

MADAME DE POMPADOUR (1721–1764)
Mistress of Louis XV

Canada is useful only to provide me with furs.

ALEXANDER POPE (1688–1744)
British poet
On Queen Caroline, consort to George II

Here lies, wrapt up in forty thousand towels,
The only proof that Caroline had bowels.

GEORGE RAFT (1895–1980)
American actor
On Mae West's first film

She stole everything but the cameras.

SALLY RAND (1904–1979)
American fan dancer
Quoted in *Newsweek*, 10 September 1979

It's better than doing needlepoint on the patio.

CONYERS READ (1881–1959)
American academic
On Queen Mary I (1516–1558)

It was her particular misfortune that the two things in the world to which she was devoted, her husband and her religion, were the two things which most estranged her from her people.

On Anne Boleyn

For something like five years she succeeded in holding him (Henry VIII) at arm's length, a remarkable performance, all things considered, and probably indicative that there was considerably more of cold calculation than of passion in Anne's attitude.

On Queen Elizabeth I

She brought England through a very perilous passage into smooth waters. Unfortunately for her successors the chart by which she steered her erratic course was destroyed with her death.

EDWARD G. ROBINSON (1893–1973)
American actor
On Ethel Barrymore

(She) . . . did what came naturally to her; took the stage, filled it, and left the rest of us to stage rear.

BERTRAND RUSSELL (1872–1970)
British philosopher
In *History of Western Philosophy*

The heroic Queen Boadicea was heading a rebellion against capitalism as represented by the philosophic apostle of austerity.

W. C. SELLAR and R. J. YEATMAN
In *1066 and All That*

The Ancient Britons, though all well over military age, painted themselves true blue or *woad*, and fought as heroically under their dashing queen, Woadicea, as they did later in thin red lines under their good queen Victoria.

WILLIAM SHAKESPEARE (1564–1616)
English playwright
In *Henry VIII*, Act II, *c.* 1613
Norfolk, speaking of Catherine of Aragon

Like a jewel, has hung twenty years
About his neck, yet never lost her lustre.

GEORGE BERNARD SHAW (1856–1950)
Irish playwright
In a letter to Marie Stopes, October 1928

I think you should insist on the separation, in the public mind, of your incidental work as a scientific critic of methods of contraception with your main profession as a teacher of matrimonial technique.

Nowadays, a parlourmaid as ignorant as Queen Victoria was when she came to the throne, would be classed as mentally defective.

On Isadora Duncan

. . . a woman whose face looked as if it had been made of sugar and someone had licked it.

DINAH SHORE (*b.* 1917)
American singer
On Bing Crosby

Bing sings like all people think they sing in the shower.

DAME EDITH SITWELL (1887–1964)
British poet
In John Lehmann's *A Nest of Tigers*

Nobody has ever been more alive than I! I am like an unpopular electric eel in a pond full of flatfish.

I have often wished I had time to cultivate modesty . . . But I am too busy thinking about myself.

SIR OSBERT SITWELL (1892–1969)
British poet
In Elisabeth Lutyens' *A Goldfish Bowl*
On composer, Dame Ethel Smyth

She would be like Richard Wagner, if only she looked a bit more feminine.

TOBIAS SMOLLETT (1721–1771)
British writer
On Anne of Cleves

The King (Henry VIII) found her so different from her picture . . . that . . . he swore they had brought him a Flanders mare.

MADAME DE STAËL (1766–1817)
French writer
In Louis de Bourrienne's *Memoirs of Napoleon Bonaparte*

Bonaparte is nothing more than a Robespierre on horseback.

RICHARD STEELE (1672–1729)
British essayist
On Elizabeth Hastings, beauty and philanthropist

Though her mien carried much more invitation than command, to behold her is an immediate check to loose behaviour, to love her is a liberal education.

ASHTON STEVENS
On Beatrice Lillie

She could make me laugh reading from the telephone book.

ADLAI STEVENSON (1900–1965)
American statesman
On Eleanor Roosevelt

Falsity withered in her presence. Hypocrisy left the room. . . . She would rather light candles than curse the darkness.

On Rose Kennedy

The woman who started it all, the head of the greatest employment agency in America.

HARRIET BEECHER STOWE (1811–1896)
American novelist
In a letter to Mrs Fallen, 1853

I am a little bit of a woman – somewhat more than forty –

about as thin and dry as a pinch of snuff; never very much to look at in my best of days, and looking like a used-up article now.

LYTTON STRACHEY (1880–1932)
British writer
On Elizabeth I

She succeeded by virtue of all the qualities which every hero should be without – dissimulation, pliability, indecision, procrastination, parsimony.

GLORIA SWANSON (1897–1983)
American film star
Quoted in *Image*, November 1971

A friend recently said, 'Just imagine *not* being famous – what would happen?' And all of a sudden I saw the face of a passer-by on the street and the oddest feeling came over me.

CHARLES MAURICE DE TALLEYRAND-PERIGORD (1754–1838)
On Madame De Staël

She is such a good friend that she would throw all her acquaintances into the water for the pleasure of fishing them out again.

ELIZABETH TAYLOR (*b.* 1932)
British-born actress
On being given the Krupp diamond by Richard Burton, 1968

I have a lust for diamonds, almost like a disease.

I've been through it all, baby. I'm Mother Courage.

SOPHIE TUCKER (1884–1966)
On herself

The last of the red-hot mamas.

I've been rich and I've been poor – rich is better.

KENNETH TYNAN (1927–1980)
British critic
On Beatrice Lillie (Lady Peel)

Her title sits on her like a halo on an anarchist.

On Greta Garbo

What, when drunk, one sees in other women, one sees in Garbo sober.

QUEEN VICTORIA (1819–1901)
In 1831

I will be good.

To Lord Clarendon, January 1855

Lord John Russell may resign, and Lord Aberdeen may resign, but I *can't* resign.

On Florence Nightingale, October 1856

Such a head! I wish we had her at the War Office.

In her Diary, 1858

21 March . . . Read to Albert out of that melancholy, interesting book, *Jane Eyre*. 4 August. At near 10 we went below and nearly finished reading that most interesting book, *Jane Eyre*. A peaceful, happy evening.

On William Gladstone, *c.* 1868

He speaks to me as if I was a public meeting.

In a letter to Disraeli, January 1878

Oh, if the Queen were a man, she would like to go and give those horrid Russians whose word one cannot trust such a beating.

In a letter to Lord Melbourne, May 1839

. . . they wished to treat me like a girl, but I will show them that I am Queen of England.

JOHN WARNER
Former husband of Elizabeth Taylor

Through Elizabeth, I have been able to better understand the plight of working women. She has described to me in vivid detail how Louis B. Mayer shouted at her when she was ten.

HORACE WALPOLE (1717–1797)
On actress, Sarah Siddons

When without motion her arms are not genteel.

BEATRICE WEBB (1881–1943)
British political writer
On Oswald Mosley

So much perfection argues rottenness somewhere.

RAQUEL WELCH (*b.* 1940)
American actress

My career started ass-backwards.

H. G. WELLS (1866–1946)
British novelist and sociologist
On social reformer, Beatrice Webb (Lady Passfield) (1858–1943)

There's no more mysticism in Beatrice than in a steam engine.

PETER WENTWORTH (1530–1596)
English parliamentarian
On Mary Stuart, Queen of Scots

The most notorious whore in all the world.

OSCAR WILDE (1854–1900)
Irish writer

Half the success of (novelist) Marie Corelli is due to the no doubt unfounded rumour that she is a woman.

The three women I have most admired are Queen Victoria, Sarah Bernhardt, and Lillie Langtry. I would have married any one of them with pleasure.

I would rather have discovered Mrs Langtry than have discovered America.

BILLY WILDER (*b.* 1906)
Film director
Quoted in *Chicago Tribune*, 16 January 1972
On the death of Marilyn Monroe

Hollywood didn't kill Marilyn Monroe; it's the Marilyn Monroes who are killing Hollywood. Marilyn was mean. Terribly mean. The meanest woman I have ever met around this town. I have never met anybody as mean as Marilyn Monroe or as utterly fabulous on the screen.

TOYAH WILLCOX (*b.* 1958)
British actress and rock singer

What I really like doing is arrogantly dropping my microphone and they scuttle on to pick it up and I go wham! smack 'em on the head. That's what audiences are there for.

THE DUCHESS OF WINDSOR (*b.* 1896)

I would like to be the head of an advertising agency.

VIRGINIA WOOLF (1882–1941)
British novelist
On James Joyce's *Ulysses*

The work of a queasy undergraduate scratching his pimples.

ALEXANDER WOOLLCOTT (1887–1943)
American journalist
On Dorothy Parker

A combination of Little Nell and Lady Macbeth

I found her in hospital typing away lugubriously. She had given her address as Bedpan Alley and represented herself as writing her way out. There was a hospital bill to pay before she dared get well.

On Mrs Patrick Campbell

She was a sinking ship firing upon her rescuers.

THE MEDIA

ADVERTISEMENT
Eve cigarettes, 1971

The first truly feminine cigarette – almost as pretty as you are. Women have been feminine since Eve, now cigarettes are feminine. Eve, also with menthol.

ADVERTISEMENT
Maidenform
Norman, Craig & Kummel

I dreamt I was Cleopatra in my Maidenform Bra.

ADVERTISEMENT
Attributed to Fay Weldon

Go to work on an egg.

ADVERTISEMENT
Palmolive soap

That schoolgirl complexion.

LINDA ALEXANDER
BBC news reader

I would hope that after three years at Newham I would be a rather more marketable commodity.

CLEVELAND AMORY (*b.* 1907)
American writer

You can't make the Duchess of Windsor into Rebecca of Sunnybrook Farm. The facts of life are very stubborn things.

BONNIE ANGELO
American journalist
On Patricia Nixon, Richard Nixon's wife

Her view of life is that of Pollyanna going steady with Horatio Alger . . . That's the way it was for her and Dick, and the America she sees agrees with her.

DIANE ARBUS (1923–1971)
American photographer

A photograph is a secret about a secret. The more it tells you the less you know.

JOAN ARMATRADING (*b.* 1947)
British singer

In America you watch TV and think that's totally unreal, then you step outside and it's just the same.

LAUREN BACALL (*b.* 1924)
American actress

If you tell the press – or anyone in Hollywood – the truth, it throws them, they don't know how to deal with it.

PEARL BAILEY (*b.* 1918)
American singer

You can taste a word.

CLARE BARNES, JR

Advertising has done more to cause the social unrest of the twentieth century than any other single factor.

MARY LOU BAX

I had to censor everything my sons watched . . . even on the Mary Tyler Moore show I heard the word *damn*!

BELFAST WOMAN
Attacking a BBC cameraman, 3 September 1972

You lying BBC: you're photographing things that aren't happening.

INGRID BERGMAN (1915–1982)
Swedish actress
On Alfred Hitchcock at his eightieth birthday dinner

A gentleman farmer who raises goose flesh.

KATE BUSH (*b.* 1958)
British singer

Whenever I see the news it's always the same depressing things. Wars, hostages and people's arms hanging off with all the tendons hanging out, y'know. So I don't tend to watch it much. I prefer to go and see a movie or something where it's all put much more poetically. People getting their heads blown off in slow motion, very beautifully.

SUE COE
British illustrator
Quoted in *The Image*, 1973

The ultimate criticism of art is the integration and application of conventional aesthetic definitions towards a silk screen of a car crash in green.

JILLY COOPER (*b.* 1937)
British writer
Quoted in *The Guardian*, 28 December 1978

If I were a grouse I'd appeal to the Brace Relations Board.

JUDITH CRIST
American film critic
On leaving halfway through an especially cloying screening . . .

My family has a history of diabetes.

ANN DICKINSON
Quoted in *Writer's Digest*, July 1978

The electric typewriter . . . is too brainy for me; it hits a letter if I breathe too hard.

EMILY DICKINSON (1830–1886)
American poet

Speech is one symptom of Affection
And Silence one –
The perfectest communication
Is heard of none.

ZELDA FITZGERALD (1900–1948)
American wife of F. Scott Fitzgerald

We grew up founding our dreams on the infinite promise of American advertising.

ANNA FORD (*b.* 1943)
British television newscaster

Let's face it, there are no plain women on television.

ELLEN FRANKFORT

Women are constantly being given double messages: society preaches purity and the media portrays women as nothing but sex objects.

ZSA ZSA GABOR (*b.* 1919)
Hungarian-born actress

Never despise what it says in the women's magazines; it may not be subtle but neither are men.

PRINCESS GRACE OF MONACO (1928–1982)

The freedom of the press works in such a way that there is not much freedom from it.

KATHERINE GRAHAM (*b.* 1917)
Publisher of the *Washington Post*

Democracy depends on information circulating freely in society.

VIRGINIA GRAHAM (*b.* 1912)
American television talkshow host

I am a living soap opera!

MEG GREENFIELD

If a politician murders his mother, the first response of the press or of his opponents will likely be not that it was a terrible thing to do, but rather that in a statement made six years before he had gone on record as being opposed to matricide.

MARGARET HALSEY (*b.* 1910)
American writer
Quoted in *Newsweek*, 17 April 1978

Identity is not found, the way Pharaoh's daughter found Moses in the bulrushes. Identity is built.

EVELYN HANSEN
Quoted in *Newsweek*, 15 May 1978

The whole message of American society – television – is you do not have to bear any discomfort.

MARION HARPER JR
American advertising executive
Quoted in *New York Herald Tribune*, 1960

Advertising is found in societies which have passed the point of satisfying the basic animal needs.

MARGOT HENTOFF (*b.* 1930)
American journalist
In *New York Herald Tribune*, 1971

Pop culture is, perhaps most of all, a culture of accessible fantasy.

KATHARINE HEPBURN (*b.* 1909)
American actress

I don't care what is written about me so long as it isn't true.

HEDDA HOPPER (1890–1966)
American gossip columnist

Nobody's interested in sweetness and light.

Being a Hollywood reporter as well as an actress I'm more or less on both sides of the fence.

GLENDA JACKSON (*b.* 1937)
British actress

Cinema criticism in the main is a total waste of everybody's time.

JINGLE, 1908
On Elinor Glyn

Would you like to sin
With Elinor Glyn
On a tiger skin?
Or would you prefer
To err with her
On some other fur?

PAULINE KAEL (*b.* 1919)
American critic

The words 'Kiss Kiss Bang Bang' which I saw on an Italian movie poster are perhaps the briefest statement imaginable of the basic appeal of the movies.

In *Newsweek*, 24 December 1973

In the arts, the critic is the only independent source of information. The rest is advertising.

When I see those ads with the quote, 'You'll have to see this picture twice', I know it's the kind of picture I don't want to see once.

SUZY KNICKERBOCKER
American journalist

As I keep repeating to anyone who will listen: there is no such thing as a secret.

DOROTHEA LANGE (1895–1965)
American photographer
In *Aperture*, 1952

Ours is a time of the machine, and ours is a need to know

that the machine can be put to creative human effort. If not, the machine can destroy us.

Bad as it is, the world is full of potentially good photographs. But to be good, photographs have to be full of the world.

In *MOMA* catalogue notes, 1966

While there is perhaps a province in which the photograph can tell us nothing more than what we see with our own eyes, there is another in which it proves to us how little our eyes permit us to see.

AMANDA LEAR
British actress

I hate to spread rumours – but what else can one do with them?

FRAN LEBOWITZ (*b. circa.* 1951)
American journalist
In *Metropolitan Life*, 1978

Radio news is bearable. This is due to the fact that while the news is being broadcast the disc jockey is not allowed to talk.

The three questions of greatest concern are: 1. Is it attractive? 2. Is it amusing? 3. Does it know its place?

The telephone is a good way to talk to people without having to offer them a drink.

ANNIE LEIBOWITZ
American photographer

Most people think that entertainers see the world. But after the twenty-sixth city, especially if you're doing one-nighters, your hotel room is your world.

C. A. LEJEUNE
British film critic
On *I Am A Camera*

Me no leica.

ANNE MORROW LINDBERGH (*b.* 1906)
American writer
In *Gift from the Sea* ('Argonauta')

Good communication is stimulating as black coffee, and just as hard to sleep after.

ANITA LOOS (*b.* 1893)
American novelist
Quoted in *The Guardian*, 1974

When the movies started delivering messages they lost their charisma. Now the messages are being replaced by porno. Between the two, porno is better.

CLARE BOOTH LUCE (*b.* 1903)
American writer and diplomat

Censorship, like charity, should begin at home; but, unlike charity, it should end there.

MARYA MANNES (*b.* 1904)
American novelist and poet
In *More in Anger*

It is television's primary damage that it provides ten million children with the same fantasy, ready-made and on a platter.

In *But Will it Sell?* ('A Word to the Wizards')

It is not enough to show people how to *live* better: there is a mandate for any group with enormous powers of communication to show people how to *be* better.

ELSA MAXWELL (1883–1963)
American socialite
In *R.S.V.P.*, 1954

I have lived by my wits all my life and I thank the Lord they are still in one, whole piece. I don't need glasses, benzedrine, or a psychiatrist . . . I can answer a city editor's four-alarm emergency and knock off a feature story or a series in time to catch a deadline.

MARGARET MEAD (1901–1978)
American anthropologist
Quoted in *Time*, 1978

For the first time the young are seeing history being made before it is censored by their elders.

LINDA MCCARTNEY
Photographer

I used to get on great with journalists until I married Paul.

MARY MCGRORY (*b.* 1918)
American journalist
Quoted in *New York Times*, 1 February 1976

To be a celebrity in America is to be forgiven everything.

MIGNON MCLAUGHLIN
American writer

No one really listens to anyone else, and if you try it for a while you'll see why.

OGDEN NASH (1902–1971)
American poet

A lady is known by the product she endorses.

SANDRA RAPHAEL
Member of Oxford English Dictonary staff
In Israel Shenker's *Words and Their Master*, 1974

Scientific jargon is superior slang.

LINDA RONSTADT (*b.* 1946)
American singer

I keep saying I wish I had as much in bed as I get in the newspapers. I'd be real busy.

NATHALIE SARRAUTE (*b.* 1902)
French writer

Television has . . . lifted the manufacture of banality out of the sphere of handicraft and placed it in that of a major industry.

EILEEN SHANAHAN

The length of a meeting rises with the square of the number of people present.

FRANK SINATRA (*b.* 1915)
American singer

The broads who work in the press are the hookers of the press. I might offer them a quick buck and a half. I'm not sure.

NANCY BANKS SMITH
British journalist
In *The Guardian*

In my experience, if you have to keep the lavatory door shut by extending your left leg, it's modern architecture.

SUSAN SONTAG (*b.* 1933)
American essayist

Life is not about significant details, illuminated in a flash, fixed for ever. Photographs are.

Today everything exists to end in a photograph.

In *New York Review of Books* ('Photography Unlimited'), 1977

Reality has come to seem more and more like what we are shown by cameras.

You can go into all sorts of situations with a camera and people will think they should serve it.

GERTRUDE STEIN (1874–1946)
American novelist

Everybody gets so much information all day long that they lose their common sense.

LILY TOMLIN (*b.* 1939)
American comedienne

If you read a lot of books, you're considered well-read. But if you watch a lot of TV, you're not considered well-viewed.

TWIGGY (Lesley Hornsby) (*b.* 1949)
British actress

If you just say nothing, there is no way they can make you talk.

ABIGAIL VAN BUREN (*b.* 1918)
American writer and journalist

People who fight fire with fire usually end up with ashes.

HARRIET VAN HORNE
American journalist
Quoted in *New York World-Telegram and Sun*, 7 June 1957

There are days when any electrical appliance in the house, including the vacuum cleaner, seems to offer more entertainment possibilities than the TV set.

BARBARA WALTERS (*b.* 1931)
American television presenter

Show me someone who never gossips, and I'll show you someone who isn't interested in people.

To co-anchor man Harry Reasoner

Unless you and I fornicate in front of everybody, people aren't going to think we get along.

BARBARA WARD
Quoted in *Saturday Review*, 30 September 1961

The modern world is not given to uncritical admiration. It expects its idols to have feet of clay, and can be reasonably sure that press and camera will report their exact dimensions.

DAME REBECCA WEST (1892–1983)
British novelist

Journalism is the ability to meet the challenge of filling space.

KATHARINE WHITEHORN
British journalist
In *Sunday Best* ('Decoding the West')

I wouldn't say when you've seen one Western you've seen the lot; but when you've seen the lot you get the feeling you've seen one.

In *Sunday Best* ('Never Never Land')

My brother cuts the time it takes to read a newspaper by skipping everything in the future tense, and it's amazing what he doesn't miss.

In *The Observer*, 1974

Worry. How pointless. I know the theory is that all this concern for the frustrated aged or forgotten Chinese children helps to change attitudes and to create at least an atmosphere in which something might happen – double beds in the geriatric ward or maybe chow mein on the school dinner menus – but I wonder if it doesn't work the other way round as well. Seeing so many tragedies that you can't do anything about may in the end simply wear the nerve-ends down so that there's no shock any more. You get used to it. You just shrug. It could be that having our withers so constantly wrung on behalf of this or that distressed group . . . has much the same effect. We get so we hardly notice any of it.

ELLEN WILKINSON (1891–1947)
British politician

I should like to help Britain to become a Third Programme country.

ANNA-MARIA WINCHESTER
Australian actress

In advertising terms, an intellectual is anybody who reads a morning newspaper.

THE ARTS

JAMES AGATE (1877–1947)
British critic and essayist
On Mrs Patrick Campbell

Her voice was like Casals' cello, and her silences had the emotional significance of Maeterlinck's shadowy speech. This was an actress who, for twenty years, had the world at her feet. She kicked it away, and the ball rolled out of her reach.

CLEVELAND AMORY (*b.* 1907)
American writer
On Marion Davies, mistress of Randolph Hearst, and aspiring movie actress.

Miss Davies had two expressions – joy and indigestion.

LAUREN BACALL (*b.* 1924)
American actress

I agree with the Bogart theory that all an actor owes the public is a good performance.

JOAN BAEZ (*b.* 1941)
American singer

It's hard to start out as an entertainer and end up as a person.

JANET BAKER (*b.* 1933)
British singer
Quoted in *Opera News*, July 1977

Singing *lieder* is like putting a piece of music under a microscope.

TALLULAH BANKHEAD (1908–1968)
American actress

On a Broadway flop

There's less in this than meets the eye.

BRIGITTE BARDOT (*b.* 1933)
French actress

A good actress lasts, but sex appeal does not.

RONA BARRETT

Pick your enemies carefully or you'll never make it in Los Angeles.

IRIS BARRY (1895–1969)
British critic

The film is a machine for seeing more than meets the eye.

ETHEL BARRYMORE (1897–1959)
American actress

For an actress to be a success she must have the face of Venus, the brains of Minerva, the grace of Terpsichore, the memory of Macaulay, the figure of Juno, and the hide of a rhinoceros.

There is as much difference between the stage and the films as between piano and a violin. Normally you can't become a virtuoso in both.

LILIAN BAYLIS (1874–1937)
British theatre manager

It is our glory that we play to the gallery, and we have a preference for a full gallery for the purpose . . . We rejoice more over the presence of one rough lad who has never heard of Shakespeare, than over the attendance of half a dozen Shakespeare students.

SIMONE DE BEAUVOIR (*b.* 1908)
French writer

Art is an attempt to integrate evil.

SARAH BERNHARDT (1844–1923)
French actress

The English are, in my opinion, the most hospitable people on earth, and they are hospitable simply and munificently. When an Englishman has opened his door to you he never closes it again. He excuses your faults and accepts your peculiarities. It is thanks to this broadness of ideas that I have been for twenty-five years the beloved and pampered artiste.

LADY BIRDWOOD
British morality campaigner
On *Oh, Calcutta!*, 1970

How long is the British taxpayer, through the Arts Council, going to finance its own moral collapse?

LOUISE BOGAN (1897–1970)
American poet

True revolutions in art restore more than they destroy.

SHIRLEY BOOTH

Actors should be overheard, not listened to, and the audience is fifty per cent of the performance.

ELIZABETH BOWEN (1899–1973)
Anglo-Irish writer
In *The Death of the Heart*

Illusions are art, for the feeling person, and it is by art that we live, if we do.

FRANCES BROOKE (1745–1789)
On Canada

I no longer wonder the elegant arts are unknown here; the rigour of the climate suspends the very powers of the understanding; what then must become of those of the imagination? . . . Genius will never mount high, where the faculties of the mind are benumbed half the year.

BRIGID BROPHY (*b.* 1929)
Irish writer
In *The Burglar*, 1967

The one consistently natural thing is to try by intelligence and imagination to improve on nature.

ELIZABETH BARRETT BROWNING (1806–1861)
British poet
In *Aurora Leigh*

Trade is art, and art's philosophy.
In Paris.

MARIA CALLAS (1923–1977)
Opera singer

When music fails to agree to the ear, to soothe the ear and the heart and the senses, then it has missed its point.

AGATHA CHRISTIE (1891–1976)
British thriller writer
On *The Mousetrap*, which opened in November 1952 and is still running.

It's a nice little play; it might run a year, eighteen months.

IRVIN S. COBB (1876–1944)
American writer
In *A Laugh A Day*
Quoting a British lady during a performance of *Antony and Cleopatra*

How different, how very different, from the home life of our own dear Queen.

SUE COLE
British illustrator
Quoted in *The Image*

Art must interfere with the normal commercial process. It must use the entertainment as a service for critical thought. That is the only hope. Art must aim at a radical change in modes of perception.

NOËL COWARD (1899–1973)
British actor and playwright

Song Title *Don't put your daughter on the stage, Mrs Worthington.*

On an unnamed actress

Her Victoria made me feel that Albert had married beneath his station.

BETTE DAVIS (*b.* 1908)
American actress

A good ham is an actor who enjoys giving pleasure to people.

The real actor – like any real artist – has a direct line to the collective heart.

SHELAGH DELANEY (*b.* 1939)
Irish playwright
In *A Taste of Honey*

The cinema has become more and more like the theatre, it's all mauling and muttering.

RUTH DRAPER (1889–1956)
American variety artiste

What is one of the lowest forms of life? . . . The earthworm – exactly! And what does he teach us? To stretch – precisely! . . . He's probably the greatest stretcher in the world!

Number seven . . . What's it meant to be, dear? . . . A 'Study'? . . . It doesn't say what of? . . . Well, that's an easy way out for an artist.

ISADORA DUNCAN (1878–1927)
American dancer

Art is not necessary at all. All that is necessary to make this world a better place to live in is to love – to love as Christ loved, as Buddha loved . . . That was the most marvellous thing about Lenin: *he* really loved mankind. Others loved themselves, money, theories, power; Lenin loved his fellow men . . . Lenin was God, as Christ was God, because God is Love and Christ and Lenin were all Love!

ELEANORA DUSE (1859–1924)
Italian actress
In A. Symons' *Studies in Seven Arts*

To save the Theatre, the Theatre must be destroyed, and actors and actresses all die of the Plague . . . they make art impossible.

BERNICE FITZGIBBON (*b.* 1897)
American businesswoman

Creativity varies inversely with the number of cooks involved in the broth.

F. SCOTT FITZGERALD (1896–1940)
American writer

To most women art is a form of scandal.

JANE FONDA (*b.* 1937)
American actress

Acting is hell: you spend all your time trying to do what they put people in asylums for.

MARGOT FONTEYN (*b.* 1919)
British ballerina

Any sort of pretension induces mediocrity in art and life alike.

ANNA FREUD (1895–1983)
Austrian-English psychoanalyst and daughter of Sigmund Freud
In 1968 annual Freud lecture to New York Psychoanalytic Society

Creative minds always have been known to survive any kind of bad training.

AMELITA GALLI-CURCI (1882–1963)
Italian opera singer

Nobody really sings in an opera. They just make loud noises.

JUDY GARLAND (1922–1969)
American actress

All you have to do is never cheat and work your best and work your hardest and they'll respond to you.

WINIFRED GAUL
German painter
In *Contemporary Artists*, 1977

Every painter who seriously dedicates himself to painting recognizes as time goes on that painting is not the chosen vehicle for making the dreams of childhood come true, for novel discoveries or inventions, or for changing society.

JEAN GIRAUDOUX (1882–1944)
French writer
In *The Apollo of Bellac*

Women have no sense of the abstract – a woman admiring the sky is a woman caressing the sky. In a woman's mind beauty is something she needs to touch.

LILIAN GISH (*b.* 1896)
American film star

What you get is a living – what you give is a life.

HANNAH GLUCKSTEIN (Gluck)
British artist
In *Contemporary Artists*, 1977

I believe that the true artist is a conduit open to any unexpected experience. There must be no preconceived ideas; variety of subject is the sign of an uninhibited spirit. All one has to do is remain faithful and undeterred to the end.

MARTHA GRAHAM (*b.* 1894)
American dancer and choreographer

The gesture is the thing truly expressive of the individual – as we think, so we will act.

It is not important that you should know what a dance means. It is only important that you should be stirred. If you can write the story of your dance it is a literary thing, but it is not dancing.

No artist is ahead of his time. He *is* his time. It is just that others are behind the time.

JANE ELLEN HARRISON (1850–1928)
In *Reminiscences of a Student's Life*

Language is as much an art and as sure a refuge as painting or music or literature.

HELEN HAYES (*b.* 1900)
American actress

Actors cannot choose the manner in which they are born – consequently it is the one gesture in their lives completely devoid of self-consciousness.

KATHARINE HEPBURN (*b.* 1909)
American actress

Life's what's important. Walking, houses, family. Birth and pain and joy. Acting's just waiting for a custard pie. That's all.

Quoted in *New York Times*, 16 January 1976

The terrible thing about acting in the theatre is that you have to do it at night.

Quoted in *Esquire*, 1967

Great performing is total simplicity, in any field, the capacity to get to the essence of it, to eliminate all the frills and all the foibles.

What acting means is that you've got to get out of your own skin.

You can't change the music of your soul.

If you give audiences a chance they'll do half your acting for you.

Acting isn't really a very high-class way to make a living, is it?

LILLIAN HELLMAN (1907–1984)
American playwright
In *Pentimento*, 1974

It is best in the theatre to act with confidence, no matter how little right you have to it.

JOSEPHINE HULL (1884–1957)
American actress

Playing Shakespeare is very tiring. You never get to sit down unless you're a king.

GLENDA JACKSON (*b.* 1937)
British actress

External rewards don't touch the continuing fascination and struggle of acting. It stays interesting because it makes increasing demands on yourself which you feel less and less able to fulfil.

ANNA JAMESON (1794–1860)
On Canada

The cold narrow minds, the confined ideas, the bygone prejudices of the society are hardly conceivable; books there are none, nor music, and as to pictures! – the Lord deliver us from such! The people do not know what a picture is.

JUDITH JAMISON

Every dancer lives on the threshold of chucking it.

SOAME JENYNS (1704–1787)
In *The Art of Dancing*

Let each fair maid, who fears to be disgraced,

Ever be sure to tie her garters fast,
Lest the loosed string amidst the public hall,
A wished-for prize to some proud fop should fall.

JAMES JOYCE (1882–1941)
Irish writer

On Lady Augusta Gregory, Irish patron of the arts, who had advertised her willingness to provide support for poets and dramatists, but was overwhelmed by the flood of applicants:

There was a kind lady called Gregory
Said, 'Come to me, poets in beggary,'
But found her imprudence
When thousands of students
Cried, 'All we are in that category.'

PAULINE KAEL (*b.* 1919)
American journalist and critic

If there's anything to learn from the history of movies, it's that corruption leads to further corruption, not to innocence.

The first prerogative of an artist in any medium is to make a fool of himself.

Movies are so rarely great art that if we cannot appreciate the great *trash* we have very little reason to be interested in them.

In *I Lost it at the Movies*

One of the surest signs of the Philistine is his reverence for the superior tastes of those who put him down.

JEAN KERR (*b.* 1923)
American author

An actor can remember his briefest notice well into senescence and long after he has forgotten his phone number and where he lives.

WANDA LANDOWSKA (1879–1959)
Polish musician

The most beautiful thing in the world is, precisely, the conjunction of learning and inspiration. Oh, the passion for research and the joy of discovery!

SUZANNE K. LANGER (*b.* 1895)
American philosopher

Art is the objectification of feeling.

AMANDA LEAR
British actress

An actress must know a little more about life than how to look good on a headsheet. An actress must know how to suffer.

ELENORE LESTER
American journalist
Quoted in *Esquire*, 1969

For an avant-garde to exist there must be an audience which, by its rigidity, challenges the artist to paint another way.

JOAN LITTLEWOOD (*b.* 1916)
British theatre director

Actors should still be called comedians – wit and inventiveness are the attributes they most need.

ALISON LURIE (*b.* 1926)
American novelist

As one went to Europe to see the living past, so one must visit Southern California to observe the future.

MARYA MANNES (*b.* 1904)
American novelist and poet

The world of sight is still limitless. It is the artist who limits vision to the cramped dimensions of his own ego.

MARY MCCARTHY (*b.* 1912)
American writer

The immense popularity of American movies abroad demonstrates that Europe is the unfinished negative of which America is the proof.

SIOBHAN MCKENNA (*b.* 1923)
Irish actress

You can do what you like in Shakespeare because people don't understand half of it anyway. But you can't in an Irish play because it really means what it says.

BETTE MIDLER (*b.* 1945)
American entertainer

So tell me about these punk rock bands. Is the *music* any good?

SYLVIA MILES
British actress

Only the untalented can afford to be humble.

AGNES DE MILLE (*b.* 1905)
American choreographer

A good education is usually harmful to a dancer. A good calf is better than a good head.

HELEN MIRREN (*b.* 1946)
British actress

Acting is such an unnatural thing to do.

JONI MITCHELL (*b.* 1943)
Canadian singer

Sorrow is so easy to express and yet so hard to tell.

MARILYN MONROE (1926–1962)
American actress

Hollywood's a place where they'll pay you a thousand dollars for a kiss, and fifty cents for your soul.

A career is born in public, talent in private.

IRIS MURDOCH (*b.* 1919)
British philosopher and writer

Art . . . is not a diversion or a side issue. It is the most educational of human activities, and a place in which the nature of morality can *be seen*.

GEORGE JEAN NATHAN (1882–1958)
American critic
In *American Mercury* ('The Theatre'), July 1926

Men go to the theatre to forget; women, to remember.

LOUISE NEVELSON (*b.* 1900)
American sculptor

It gave me great pleasure to think that I could take wood, make it good, and make people like Rockefeller buy it with paper money.

JEAN MARY NORMAN

Art is the difference between seeing and just identifying.

LORD OLIVIER (*b.* 1907)
British actor

We used to have actresses trying to become stars; now we have stars trying to become actresses.

YOKO ONO (*b.* 1934)
Japanese artist

All my concerts had no sounds in them: they were completely silent . . . People had to make their own music in their minds.

DOROTHY PARKER (1893–1967)
American writer and wit

Art is a form of catharsis.

ANN PETRY (*b.* 1912)
American writer

All truly great art is propaganda.

VANESSA REDGRAVE (*b.* 1937)
British actress

The stage is actor's country. You have to get your passport stamped every so often or they take away your citizenship.

KATE REID
Canadian actress

Acting is not being emotion, but being able to express emotion.

AGNES REPPLIER (1858–1950)
American essayist

Art is never didactic, does not take kindly to facts, is helpless to grapple with theories, and is killed outright by a sermon.

GINGER ROGERS (*b.* 1911)
American film star

There are no small parts. Only small actors.

LINDA RONSTADT (*b.* 1946)
American singer

Your attitude to your audience should be that they're a bunch of non-believers and you're the only person that could convince them.

FRANÇOISE SAGAN (*b.* 1936)
French novelist

Art must take reality by surprise. It takes those moments which are for us merely a moment, plus a moment, plus another moment, and arbitrarily transforms them into a special series of moments held together by a major emotion.

The illusion of art is to make one believe that great literature is very close to life, but exactly the opposite is true. Life is amorphous, literature is formal.

ADELA ROGERS ST JOHN (*b.* 1894)
American writer

The silent stars moved silently, especially Gary Cooper, who came from the Great Open Spaces where men *were* silent.

DOROTHY L. SAYERS (1893–1957)
British author
In *The Unpleasantness at the Bellona Club*, 1928

Tragedy can be turned into comedy by sitting down.

GEORGE BERNARD SHAW (1856–1950)
Irish playwright

Quoted in *Saturday Review*, 7 March 1896

You will tell me no doubt that Mrs Patrick Campbell cannot act. Who said she could? Who wants her to act? Who cares twopence whether she possesses that or any other second-rate accomplishment? On the highest plane one does not act, one *is*.

In a letter to Mrs Patrick Campbell, 19 December 1938

If only you could write a true book entitled WHY, THOUGH I WAS A WONDERFUL ACTRESS, NO MANAGER OR AUTHOR WOULD EVER ENGAGE ME TWICE IF HE COULD POSSIBLY HELP IT, it would be a bestseller. But you couldn't. Besides, you don't know. I do.

SIMONE SIGNORET (*b.* 1921)
French actress

The body of an actor is like a well in which experiences are stored, then tapped when needed.

PATTI SMITH (*b.* 1946)
American singer

Rock 'n' roll is dream soup, what's your brand?

DAME ETHEL SMYTH (1858–1944)
British composer and suffragette

It was generous-minded Sir Henry Wood who first started mixed bathing in the sea of music.

SUSAN SONTAG (*b.* 1933)
American essayist

Real art has the capacity to make us nervous. By reducing the work of art to its content and then interpreting *that*, one tames the work of art.

The camera makes everyone a tourist in other people's reality, and eventually in one's own.

Science fiction films are not about science; they are about disaster, one of the oldest subjects of art.

The Happening operates by creating an asymmetrical network of surprises, without climax of consummation: this is the alogic of dreams rather than the logic of most art.

Art (and art-making) is a form of consciousness; the materials of art are the variety of forms of consciousness.

The history of the arts is tantamount to the discovery and formulation of a repertory of objects on which to lavish attention.

The moral pleasure in art, as well as the moral service that art provides, consists in the intelligent gratification of consciousness.

MADAME DE STAËL (1766–1817)
French writer
In *Corinne*, 1807

Music revives the recollections it would appease.

STELLA STEVENS (*b.* 1938)
American actress

I think naked people are very nice. Posing in the nude is perhaps the best way of reaching people.

GLORIA SWANSON (1897–1983)
American film star

All creative people should be required to leave California for three months every year.

DAME ELLEN TERRY (1874–1928)
In letters to George Bernard Shaw

Do you know, I have no weight on the stage; unless I have heavy robes I can't keep on the ground.

I generally go and see Burne-Jones when there's a fog. He looks so angelic, painting away there by candlelight.

LILY TOMLIN (*b.* 1939)
American comedienne

If you can't be direct, why be?

TWIGGY (Lesley Hornsby) (*b.* 1949)
British actress

I always loved the Beatles. They were incredible. I remember having a fight in class with a girl who tore down her Beatles pictures when Dave Clark came along. I didn't speak to her for three weeks.

It's not a matter of playing the right notes, is it. It's a feel.

LIV ULLMANN (*b.* 1939)
Norwegian actress

My breasts aren't actresses.

DAME NINETTE DE VALOIS (*b.* 1898)
British dancer and choreographer

You cannot create genius. All you can do is nurture it.

THELMA VOTIPKA
Opera singer
Quoted in *New York Times*, 27 October 1972

The prima donna's dressing-room is the one nearest the exit.

CREIGHTON WEBB
In answer to a woman who said of opera star, Geraldine Farrer, 'My, aren't her ankles big!'

Madame, she doesn't sing with her ankles.

SIMONE WEIL (1909–1943)
French writer
In *The Need for Roots*

Culture is an instrument wielded by professors to manufacture professors, who, when their turn comes, will manufacture professors.

MAE WEST (1892–1980)
American film star

Hiring someone to write your autobiography is like paying someone to take a bath for you.

EDITH WHARTON (1862–1937)
American novelist
In *The Age of Innocence*

An unalterable and unquestioned law of the musical world required that the German text of French operas sung by Swedish artists should be translated into Italian for the clearer understanding of English-speaking audiences.

SHELLEY WINTERS (*b.* 1922)
American actress

Acting is like painting pictures on bathroom tissues. Ten minutes later you throw them away and they are gone.

LITERATURE

MARTHA ALBRAND (*b.* 1912)
American crime writer

All writing is a process of elimination.

LOUISA MAY ALCOTT (1832–1888)
American novelist

My definition (of a philosopher) is of a man up on a balloon, with his family and friends holding the ropes which confine him to earth and trying to haul him down.

In Katharine Anthony's *Louisa May Alcott*

When I don't look like the tragic muse, I look like a smoky relic of the great Boston Fire.

MAYA ANGELOU (*b.* 1928)
American writer

I intend to become America's black female Proust.

KATHERINE ANTHONY (1917–1965)
American writer

To the biographer, all lives bar none are dramatic constructions.

JANE ARDEN
British dramatist

Quoted in *Contemporary Dramatists*, 1977

Reading can be as paralyzing an act (even absorbing so-called erudite works) as bingo, if the information does not recreate the being and radicalize the behaviour. There are no such things as creative writers – some people have better radio sets for tuning in to the only creation. The world needs healers, not 'artists'.

HANNAH ARENDT
(1906–1975)
German-born political philosopher

Action without a name, a 'who' attached to it, is meaningless.

Poets are the only people to whom love is not only a crucial, but an indispensable experience, which entitles them to mistake it for a universal one.

JANE AUSTEN (1775–1817)
British novelist

In *Emma*

One half of the world cannot understand the pleasures of the other.

In a letter to Anna Austen, 28 September 1814

Walter Scott has no business to write novels, especially good ones. It is not fair – He has Fame and Profit enough as a Poet, and should not be taking the bread out of other people's mouths. I do not like him, & do not mean to like *Waverley* if I can help it – but fear I must.

In a letter to the Rev. James Clarke, 1815

I think I may boast myself to be, with all possible vanity, the most unlearned and uninformed female who ever dared to be an authoress.

ENID BAGNOLD (*b.* 1889)
British writer
Quoted in *Contemporary Novelists*, 1976

Inside the brain there's a kind of instrument, never quite learned and most *un*fully played . . .

BERYL BAINBRIDGE (*b.* 1934)
British writer
Quoted in *Contemporary Novelists*, 1976

Once the grammar has been learned [writing] is simply talking on paper and in time learning what not to say.

MARGARET C. BANNING (*b.* 1891)
American novelist

Fiction is not a dream. Nor is it guesswork. It is imagining based on facts, and the facts must be accurate or the work of imagining will not stand up.

SIMONE DE BEAUVOIR (*b.* 1908)
French writer
In *The Second Sex*

The original writer, as long as he isn't dead, is always scandalous.

In *La Force de l'Age*

Writing is a *métier* . . . that one learns by writing.

BRIDGET BOLAND (*b.* 1913)
Irish playwright

In the end every play is saying 'Belief is dangerous'.

PHYLLIS BOTTOME (1882–1963)
American crime writer

If a writer is true to his characters they will give him his plot. Observations must play second fiddle to integrity.

RICHARD BRIDGEMAN
In *Gertrude Stein in Pieces*

Reading Gertrude Stein at length is not unlike making one's way through an interminable and badly printed game book.

CHARLOTTE BRONTË (1816–1855)
British novelist
In *Jane Eyre*

Prejudices, it is well known, are most difficult to eradicate from the heart whose soil has never been loosened or fertilized by education; they grow there, firm as weeds among stones.

In a letter to W. S. Williams, 1850
On Jane Austen

Her business is not half so much with the human heart as with the human eye, mouth, hands and feet. . . . Jane Austen was a complete and most sensible lady, but a very incomplete and rather insensible (*not senseless*) woman. If this is heresy, I cannot help it.

BRIGID BROPHY (*b.* 1929)
Irish writer
In *In Transit*

The thriller is the cardinal twentieth-century form. All it, like the twentieth century, wants to know is: Who's Guilty?

In *Don't Ever Forget*
On Jane Austen

Her books are domestic in the sense that *Oedipus Rex* is domestic. Her moral dilemmas are often drawn in precisely oedipal terms.

On Ivy Compton-Burnett

To my sense Miss Compton-Burnett is not exactly an artist. She is something less valuable but rarer – the inventor of a wholly original species of puzzle. . . . Reading them [her novels] is like playing some Monopoly for Intellectuals, in which you can buy, as well as houses and hotels, plaques to set up on them recording that a great writer once lived there.

ELIZABETH BARRETT BROWNING (1806–1861)
British poet
In *Aurora Leigh*

Books succeed,
And lives fail.

ROBERT BROWNING (1812–1889)
British poet
On his wife in a letter to Isa Blagden, 18 August 1871

The simple truth is that *she* was the poet, and I the clever person by comparison.

FANNY BURNEY (Madame D'Arblay) (1752–1840)
British novelist and diarist
In *Evelina*

Now I am ashamed of confessing that I have nothing to confess.

HORTENSE CALISHER (*b.* 1911)
American novelist

Not yet published a writer lies in the womb . . . waiting for the privilege to breathe. Outside is the great, exhaling company of those who have expressed.

First publication is a pure, carnal leap into that dark which one dreams is life.

JANE WELSH CARLYLE (1801–1866)
Wife of Thomas Carlyle
In a letter to Helen Walsh, March 1843
On Jane Austen

Too washy; water-gruel for mind and body at the same time were too bad.

In her *Journal*, 21 November 1855

When one has been threatened with a great injustice, one accepts a smaller as a favour.

In a letter, 17 May 1849
On Mrs Elizabeth Gaskell

A natural unassuming woman whom they have been doing their best to spoil by making a lioness of her.

LEWIS CARROLL (Charles Lutwidge Dodgson) (1832–1898)
British mathematician and writer
In *Alice's Adventures in Wonderland*

'What is the use of a book,' thought Alice, 'without pictures or conversations?'

ANGELA CARTER (*b.* 1940)
British writer
Quoting Melville on *Moby Dick* about her own book, *The Sadeian Woman*

I have written a very wicked story and I feel pure as a lamb.

BARBARA CARTLAND
British romantic novelist

A historical romance is the only kind of book where chastity really counts.

'Sayings of the Week' (*Observer*, 20 June 1976)

I'll wager you that in ten years it will be fashionable again to be a virgin.

G. K. CHESTERTON (1874–1936)
British essayist and novelist
On Charlotte Brontë

She showed that abysses may exist inside a governess and eternities inside a manufacturer.

AGATHA CHRISTIE (1891–1976)
British thriller writer

The best time for planning a book is while you're doing the dishes.

It is completely unimportant. That is why it is so interesting.

I've always believed in writing without a collaborator, because where two people are writing the same book, each believes he gets all the worries and only half the royalties.

COLETTE (Sidonie-Gabrielle) (1873–1954)
French writer

What a wonderful life I've had! I only wish I'd realized it sooner.

In Dorothea Straus' *Showcases*

Happiness? Come, what should I do with it?

In *Earthly Paradise* ('The Occupation')

To a poet, silence is an acceptable response, even a flattering one.

('The South of France')

As for an authentic villain, the real thing, the absolute, the artist, one rarely meets him even once in a lifetime. The ordinary bad hat is always in part a decent fellow.

('The Footwarmer')

When one can read, can penetrate the enchanted realm of books, why write?

CATHERINE COOKSON (*b.* 1906)
British novelist

The way I look at it I cast my bread upon the waters and I got a baker's shop back.

EMILY DICKINSON (1830–1886)
American poet

If . . . it makes my whole body so cold no fire can warm me, I know that is poetry.

Tell the truth
But tell it slant.

The Truth must dazzle gradually
Or every man be blind.

MARY ABIGAIL DODGE (Gail Hamilton) (1838–1896)
In *Country Living and Country Thinking* (Preface)

Whatever an author puts between the two covers of his book is public property; whatever of himself he does not put there is his private property, as much as if he had never written a word.

MARGARET DRABBLE (*b.* 1939)
British novelist
In *A Summer Bird-Cage*

Perhaps the rare and simple pleasure of being seen for what one is compensates for the misery of being it.

LAWRENCE DURRELL (*b.* 1912)
British writer
In *Justine*

There are only three things to be done with a woman. You can love her, suffer for her, or turn her into literature.

GEORGE ELIOT (Marian Evans) (1819–1880)
British novelist

There are characters which are continually creating collisions and nodes for themselves in dramas which nobody is prepared to act with them.

In *Felix Holt*

A woman's hopes are woven of sunbeams, a shadow annihilates them.

In a letter to Charles Bray, 11 June 1848

I have read *Jane Eyre* . . . and shall be glad to know what you admire in it. All self-sacrifice is good – but one would like it to be in a somewhat nobler cause than that of a diabolical law which chains a man body and soul to a putrefying carcase.

In a letter to John Blackwood, 4 February 1857

Whatever may be the success of my stories, I shall be resolute in preserving my incognito, having observed that a *nom de plume* secures all the advantages without the disagreeables of reputation. Perhaps, therefore, it will be well to give you my prospective name . . . I shall subscribe myself, best and most sympathizing of editors, Yours very truly, George Eliot.

In a letter to Alexander Main, 11 September 1871

I have the conviction that excessive literary production is a social offence.

RALPH WALDO EMERSON (1803–1882)
American writer
In his *Journal*
On the novels of Jane Austen

I am at a loss to understand why people hold [them] at so high a rate, which seem to me vulgar in tone, sterile in artistic invention . . . without genius, wit or knowledge of the world.

On Harriet Beecher Stowe's *Uncle Tom's Cabin*

We have seen an American woman write a novel of which a million copies were sold in all languages, and which had one merit, of speaking to the universal heart.

CLIFTON FADIMAN (*b.* 1904)
American essayist
On Gertrude Stein

[She] was a past master in making nothing happen very slowly.

EDNA FERBER (1887–1968)
American writer and playwright

Life cannot defeat a writer who is in love with writing – for life itself is a writer's lover until death.

FLORENCE KIPPER FRANK
Quoted in *Morrow's Almanac*, 1929

The canny among the publishers know that an enormous popular appetite for the insulting of the famous must be gratified, and the modern biographer emerges from the editorial conference a sadist and a wiser man.

MRS HUGH FRASER
On Elizabeth Barrett Browning

The poetess was everything I did not like. . . . She never

laughed or even smiled once, during the whole conversation. . . . I was glad when I got out into the sunshine again.

MARGARET FULLER (1810–1850)
American writer and critic
In *Summer on the Lakes*

Our desires, once realised, haunt us again less readily.

No temple can still the personal griefs and strifes in the breasts of its visitors.

MRS ELIZABETH GASKELL (1810–1865)
British novelist
In *Cranford*

One gives people in grief their own way.

A little credulity helps one on through life very smoothly.

STELLA GIBBONS (*b.* 1902)
British novelist
In *Cold Comfort Farm*

Something nasty in the woodshed.

LADY GREGORY (1852–1932)
Irish playwright
In William Butler Yeats' *Journal*, 17 March 1909

Tennyson had the British Empire for God, and Queen Victoria for Virgin Mary.

DOROTHY FRANCES GURNEY (1858–1932)
In *God's Garden*

The kiss of the sun for pardon,
  The song of the birds for mirth,
One is nearer God's Heart in a garden
  Than anywhere else on earth.

MARGARET HALSEY (*b.* 1910)
American writer
In *With Malice Toward Some*

Through all the shrines (at Stratford-on-Avon) surge English and American tourists, either people who have read too much Shakespeare at the expense of good, healthy detective stories or people who have never read him at all and hope to get the same results by bumping their heads on low beams.

LILLIAN HELLMAN (1907–1984)
American playwright

Nothing you write, if you hope to be good, will ever come out as you first hoped.

Quoted in *New York Times*, 21 February 1960

They're fancy talkers about themselves, writers. If I had to give young writers advice, I would say don't listen to writers talking about writing or themselves.

Quoted in *Writers at Work* (3rd Series), 1967

The writer's intention hasn't anything to do with what he achieves. The intent to earn money or the intent to be famous or the intent to be great doesn't matter in the end. Just what comes out.

In *An Unfinished Woman*

Intellectuals can tell themselves anything, sell themselves any bill of goods, which is why they were so often patsies for the ruling classes.

FELICIA DOROTHEA HEMANS (1793–1835)
British poet
In *Casablanca*

The boy stood on the burning deck
Whence all but he had fled;
The flame that lit the battle's wreck
Shone round him o'er the dead.

KATHARINE HEPBURN (*b.* 1909)
American actress

A book is only your point of view.

PENELOPE HOUSTON (1828–1909)
British novelist
On Agatha Christie

At her best, [her] writing is instantly forgettable; at her worst, she may have forgotten it instantly herself.

MARY HOWITT (1799–1888)
British author

'Will you walk into my parlour?' said a spider to a fly: ' 'Tis the prettiest little parlour that ever you did spy.'

ERICA JONG (*b.* 1942)
American writer
Quoted in William Packard's *The Craft of Poetry*

Writing is one of the few professions left where you take all the responsibility for what you do. It's really dangerous and ultimately destroys you as a writer if you start thinking about responses to your work or what your audience needs.

GLORIA KATZ
American scriptwriter
In *New York Times*, 1975

How can you write anything topical when it takes three years to make it?

ROSMARIE WITTMAN LAMB
Quoted in *New York Times*, 22 June 1975

Novels, when well-written, tell you more about life than the most sophisticated computerized sociology.

FRAN LEBOWITZ (*b. circa* 1951)
American journalist

Having been unpopular in high school is not just cause for book publication.

ADA LEVERSON (1862–1933)
In *Love at Second Sight*

People were not charmed with Eglantine because she herself was charming, but because she was charmed.

In *The Twelfth Hour*

'No hurry, no hurry,' said Sir James, with that air of self-denial that conveys the urgent necessity of intense speed.

SINCLAIR LEWIS (1885–1951)
American novelist

Harriet Beecher Stowe. . . . whose *Uncle Tom's Cabin* was the first evidence to America that no hurricane can be so disastrous to a country as a ruthlessly humanitarian woman.

ANN MORROW LINDBERGH (*b.* 1906)
American writer
In *Locked Rooms and Open Doors*

I must write it all out, at any cost. Writing is thinking. It is more than living, for it is being conscious of living.

CLARE BOOTHE LUCE (*b.* 1903)
American writer and diplomat
Quoted in *Vanity Fair*, October 1930

Lying increases the creative faculties, expands the ego, lessens the friction of social contacts . . . it is only in lies, wholeheartedly and bravely told, that human nature attains through words and speech the forbearance, the nobility, the romance, the idealism, that – being what it is – it falls so short of in fact and in deed.

ROSE MACAULAY (1889–1958)
British novelist

It was a book to kill time for those who like it better dead.

BETTY MACDONALD (*d.* 1958)
American writer
In *The Egg and I*

The days slipped down like junket, leaving no taste on the tongue.

W. SOMERSET MAUGHAM (1874–1965)
British writer
On Jane Austen

Nothing very much happens in her books, and yet, when you come to the bottom of a page, you eagerly turn it to learn what will happen next.

DAPHNE DU MAURIER (*b.* 1907)
British novelist

Writers should be read – but neither seen nor heard.

MARY MCCARTHY (*b.* 1912)
American writer
In *On the Contrary* ('Characters in Fiction')

Others are to us like the 'characters' in fiction, eternal and incorrigible; the surprises they give us turn out in the end to have been predictable – unexpected variations on the theme of being themselves.

On Ivy Compton-Burnett

One of the mischievous originalities of Compton-Burnett is to have pursued this insular tendency to the extreme, making it her trademark. . . . She has no imitators. The formula is a trade secret.

MIGNON MCLAUGHLIN
American writer

If you jot down every silly thought that pops into your mind, you will soon find out everything you most seriously believe.

GRACE METALIOUS (1924–1964)
Author of *Peyton Place*

I'm a lousy writer; a helluva lot of people have got lousy taste.

EDNA ST VINCENT MILLAY (1892–1950)
American poet

A person who publishes a book wilfully appears before the public with his pants down.

NANCY MITFORD (1904–1973)
British writer
In *The Pursuit of Love*

I have only read one book in my life, and that is *White Fang*. It's so frightfully good I've never bothered to read another.

LADY MARY MONTAGU (1689–1762)
English letter writer
In *To the Imitator of the First Satire of Horace*

Satire should, like a polished razor keen,
Wound with a touch that's scarcely felt or seen.

MARIANNE MOORE (1887–1972)
American poet
Quoted in *Writers at Work* (2nd Series)

A writer is unfair to himself when he is unable to be hard on himself.

On accepting the National Book Award

I see no reason for calling my work poetry except that there is no other category in which to put it.

IRIS MURDOCH (*b.* 1919)
British philosopher and novelist
In *The Black Prince*

Writing is like getting married. One should never commit oneself until one is amazed at one's luck.

CYNTHIA OZICK

Stories ought to judge and interpret the world.

GRACE PALEY (*b.* 1922)
American writer
Quoted in *Ms*, 1974

Literature, fiction, poetry, whatever, makes justice in the world. That's why it almost always has to be on the side of the underdog.

DOROTHY PARKER (1893–1967)
American writer and wit

English authors write better than Americans – and Irish authors write better than anybody.

If you're going to write, don't pretend to write down. It's going to be the best you can do, and it's the fact that it's the best you can do that kills you.

On lady novelists

As artists they're rot, but as providers they're oil wells – they gush.

SYLVIA PLATH (1932–1963)
American poet

Nothing stinks like a pile of unpublished writing.

The blood jet is poetry
There is no stopping it.

In *Wintering*

Winter is for women –
The woman still at her knitting,
At the cradle of Spanish walnut,
Her body a bulb in the cold and too dumb to think.

KATHERINE ANNE PORTER (1890–1930)
American writer

No man can be explained by his personal history, least of all a poet.

Most people won't realise that writing is a craft. You have to take your apprenticeship in it like anything else.

BEATRIX POTTER (1866–1943)
English writer of children's stories
To her cousin, Ulla Hyde Parker

You are Danish by birth; you share your nationality with Hans Christian Andersen . . . my children's stories will one day be as famous and as much read as his.

PETER S. PRESCOTT
Quoted in *Newsweek*, 30 May 1977

Many books today suggest that the mass of women lead lives of noisy desperation.

MRS ANNA ROSS
In a letter to Lord Ponsonby, 1910

I don't believe in publishers who wish to butter their bannocks on both sides while they'll hardly allow an author to smell treacle. I consider they are too grabby together and like Methodists they love to keep the Sabbath and everything else they can lay their hands on.

FRANCOISE SAGAN (*b.* 1936)
French novelist

Writing is just having a sheet of paper, a pen and not a shadow of an idea of what you're going to say.

NATHALIE SARRAUTE (*b.* 1902)
French writer

Poetry is what makes the invisible appear.

DAME EDITH SITWELL (1887–1964)
British poet
'Sayings of the Week' (*The Observer*, 13 May 1923)

A great many people now reading and writing would be better employed in keeping rabbits.

In *Vogue* ('Some Observations on Women's Poetry'), 1925

Women's poetry should, above all things, be elegant as a peacock, and there should be a fantastic element, a certain strangeness in its beauty. But above all, let us avoid sentimentality: do not let us write about Pierrot, or Arcady, or how much good we should like to do in the world!

In a letter to Maurice Bowra, 24 January 1944

It is a dangerous thing to say, but I can say it to you. Sometimes, when I begin a poem, it is almost like automatic writing. Then I use my mind on it afterwards.

Quoted in *Life*, 1963

Poetry is the deification of reality.

STEVIE SMITH (1902–1971)
British poet
In *Selected Poems* ('My Muse')

Why does my Muse only speak when she is unhappy?
She does not, I only listen when I am unhappy
When I am happy I live and despise writing
For my Muse this cannot but be dispiriting.

SUSAN SONTAG (*b.* 1933)
American essayist

Books are . . . funny little portable pieces of thought.

Perversity is the muse of modern literature.

GERTRUDE STEIN (1874–1946)
American writer

A Rose is a Rose is a Rose.

Hemingway's remarks are not literature.

Anything one is remembering is a repetition, but existing as a human being, that is being, listening and hearing is never repetition.

HARRIET BEECHER STOWE (1811–1896)
American writer, author of *Uncle Tom's Cabin*

I no more thought of style or literary excellence than the

mother who rushes into the street and cries for help to save her children from a burning house, thinks of the teachings of the rhetorician or the elocutionist.

JACQUELINE SUSANN (1921–1974)
American novelist

I've made characters live, so that people talk about them at cocktail parties, and that, to me, is what counts.

MARK TWAIN (Samuel Langhorne Clemens) (1835–1910)

When I take up one of Jane Austen's books . . . I feel like a barkeeper entering the kingdom of heaven . . . He would not find the place to his taste, and he would probably say so.

ANNE TYLER (*b.* 1931)
American writer

My family can always tell when I'm well into a novel because the meals get very crummy.

MRS HUMPHRY WARD (1851–1920)
British novelist
On Charlotte Brontë

Then, as to the Celtic pride, the Celtic shyness, the Celtic endurance, Charlotte Brontë was rich in them all.

DAME REBECCA WEST (1892–1983)
British novelist

Just how difficult it is to write biography can be reckoned by anybody who sits down and considers just how many people know the real truth about his or her love affairs.

E. B. WHITE (*b.* 1899)
American essayist and journalist
On his wife, Katharine S. White

She would write eight or ten words, then draw her gun and shoot them down.

ETHEL WILSON (*b.* 1890)
Canadian novelist

A writer's mind seems to be situated partly in the solar plexus and partly in the head.

VIRGINIA WOOLF (1882–1941)
British novelist

I am reading Henry James . . . and feel myself as one entombed in a block of smooth amber.

Biography is to give a man some kind of shape after his death.

The test of a book (to a writer) is if it makes a space in which, quite naturally, you can say what you want to say.

In *The Waves*

I have lost friends, some by death . . . others through sheer inability to cross the street.

In *A Room of One's Own*

It is in our idleness, in our dreams, that the submerged truth sometimes comes to the top.

If woman had no existence save in the fiction written by men, one would imagine her a person of the utmost importance; very various; heroic and mean; splendid and sordid; infinitely beautiful and hideous in the extreme; as great as a man, some think even greater.

Literature is strewn with the wreckage of men who have minded beyond reason the opinion of others.

Masterpieces are not single and solitary births; they are the outcome of many years of thinking in common, of thinking by the body of the people, so that the experience of the mass is behind the single voice.

In *The Common Reader*
On Charlotte Brontë

She does not attempt to solve the problems of human life, she is even unaware that such problems exist; all her force, and it is the more tremendous for being constricted, goes into the assertion, 'I love', 'I hate', 'I suffer'.

A good essay must have this permanent quality about it; it must draw its curtain round us, but it must be a curtain that shuts us in not out.

On 'Modern Fiction'

Life is not a series of gig lamps symmetrically arranged; life is a luminous halo, a semi-transparent envelope surrounding us from the beginning of consciousness to the end.

On George Eliot

Middlemarch, the magnificent book which with all its imperfections is one of the few English novels for grown-up people.

In a letter to Lytton Strachey

I read the book of Job last night – I don't think God comes well out of it.

WIT

JANE ACE (1905–1974)
American actress

Time wounds all heels.

The chickens have come home to roast.

LISA ALTHER (*b.* 1944)
American novelist
In *Kinflicks*

I've always felt that a person's intelligence is directly reflected by the number of conflicting points of view he can entertain simultaneously on the same topic.

MARIE ARAGON

We sold our house and are moving into one of those pandemoniums.

ANNE ARMSTRONG (*b.* 1927)
American politician and diplomat

In the space age the most important space is between the ears.

MARGOT ASQUITH (1865–1945)
British society hostess
On an unnamed US general

An imitation rough diamond.

On an unnamed friend

She's as tough as an ox. She'll be turned into Bovril when she dies.

Margot,' said Jean Harlow, stressing the final 't', 'how lovely to see you.'

'No, dear,' Lady Asquith replied, 'the *t* is silent as in Harlow.'

To her hostess as she left a party

Don't think it hasn't been charming, because it hasn't.

The trouble with Lord Birkenhead is that he is so un-Christlike.

His modesty amounts to a deformity.

LADY ASTOR (1879–1964)
First woman MP

On being asked by a heckler how many toes has a pig's foot

Take off your boots, man, and count for yourself.

JANE AUSTEN (1775–1817)
British novelist
In *Mansfield Park*

If this man had not twelve thousand a year, he would be a very stupid fellow.

HYLDA BAKER (*b.* 1909)
British comedienne

Punctuality is something that if you have it, there's often no one around to share it with you.

TALLULAH BANKHEAD (1902–1968)
American actress

Cocaine isn't habit-forming. I should know – I've been using it for years.

The only thing I regret about my past is the length of it. If I had to live my life again, I'd make the same mistakes, only sooner.

BINNIE BARNES (*b.* 1906)
British actress

He's the kind of bore who's here today and here tomorrow.

LOUISE BEAL

Love thy neighbour as thyself – but choose your neighbourhood.

QUEEN CAROLINE (1683–1737)
Wife of George II

On her deathbed she tried to persuade her husband to remarry. But he refused, saying, 'Never. I will always take mistresses.'

'That shouldn't hamper your marrying,' she answered.

CHARLOTTE BINGHAM (*b.* 1942)
British writer
In L. & M. Cowan's *The Wit of Women*

A twenty-five-year-old virgin is like the man who was set upon by thieves – everyone passes by.

BRIGID BROPHY (*b.* 1929)
Irish writer

An airport is a free-range womb.

CORAL BROWNE (*b.* 1913)
Australian-born actress

On being told there was no part suitable for her first husband in a production of King Lear she refused to take no for an answer and after searching painstakingly through the text triumphantly came up with the stage direction 'A Camp near Dover'.

Commenting on the unlikely affair between a distinguished elderly actor and an aspiring young actress, 'I never understood what he saw in her until I saw her eating corn on the cob at the Caprice.'

MRS PATRICK CAMPBELL (1865–1940)
British actress

It doesn't matter what you do in the bedroom as long as you don't do it in the street and frighten the horses.

LADY VIOLET BONHAM CARTER (1887–1969)
British politician

Tories are not always wrong, but they are always wrong at the right moment.

On comparing Lloyd George and Bonar Law

We have to choose between one man suffering from St Vitus's Dance and another from sleeping sickness.

JOYCE CARY (1888–1957)
British novelist
In *The Horse's Mouth*

Sara could commit adultery at one end and weep for her sins at the other, and enjoy both operations at once.

ILKA CHASE (*b.* 1905)
American writer and actress

If Dorothy Thompson doesn't know as much as God, she most certainly knows as much as He did at her age.

PHYLLIS DILLER (*b.* 1917)
American comedienne

Never go to bed mad. Stay up and fight.

Living in Hollywood is like living in a lit cigar butt.

ELEANOR DOAN

The brain is as strong as its weakest think.

Love your enemy – it will drive him nuts.

SUE DYTRI

Tact: Tongue in check.

SUSAN ERTZ (*b. circa.* 1894)
American novelist

Millions long for immortality who do not know what to do with themselves on a rainy Sunday afternoon.

He talked with more claret than clarity.

ZSA ZSA GABOR (*b.* 1919)
Hungarian-born actress

To a smart girl men are no problem – they're the answer.

A man in love is incomplete until he has married. Then he's finished.

Macho does not prove mucho.

HERMIONE GINGOLD (*b.* 1897)
British actress

I've discovered that what we in England call draughts you in America call cross-ventilation.

AGNES GUILFOYLE
On confession

Good for the soul – but bad for the heel.

MARGAUX HEMINGWAY (*b.* 1962)
American model

Big girls need big diamonds.

LILLIAN HELLMAN (1907–1984)
American playwright

Cynicism is an unpleasant way of saying the truth.

FANNIE HURST (1889–1968)
American novelist

When the mind's eye turns inwards, it blazes upon the dearly beloved image of oneself.

KAY INGRAM

Women prefer men to have something tender about them – especially the legal kind.

GLYNIS JOHNS (*b.* 1923)
British actress

I think the Swiss have sublimated their sense of time into clock-making.

JEAN KERR (*b.* 1923)
American author

The average, healthy, well-adjusted adult gets up at 7.30 in the morning feeling just plain terrible.

I feel about airplanes the way I feel about diets. It seems to me that they are wonderful things for other people to go on.

DOROTHY KILGALLEN

Doorman – a genius who can open the door of your car with one hand, help you in with the other, and still have one left for the tip.

DORIS KING
On Beverly Sills, the opera singer

Isn't Beverly Sills a suburb of Los Angeles?

ANN LANDERS (*b.* 1918)
American journalist

One out of four people in this country is mentally imbalanced. Think of your three closest friends – and if they seem okay, then you're the one.

Television has proved that people will look at anything rather than each other.

MARY WILSON LITTLE
American writer

A youth with his first cigar makes himself sick; a youth with his first girl makes other people sick.

The tombstone is about the only thing that can stand upright and lie on its face at the same time.

MARIE LLOYD (1870–1922)
British music-hall artist

A little of what you fancy does you good.

ANITA LOOS (*b.* 1893)
American novelist

I think money is on the way out.

Quoted in *International Herald Tribune*, 1973

On a plane you can pick up more and better people than on any other public conveyance since the stagecoach.

ANNIE LOTH

It looks like a flaw in the ointment.

CLARE BOOTH LUCE (*b.* 1903)
American writer and diplomat

Like using a guillotine to cure dandruff.

Nature abhors a virgin – a frozen asset.

No good deed will go unpunished.

MAE MALOO
Quoted in *Reader's Digest*, September 1976

There's one thing to be said for inviting trouble; it generally accepts.

DAPHNE DU MAURIER (*b.* 1907)
British novelist
On her house

It . . . was full of dry rot. An unkind visitor said the only reason Menabilly still stood was that the woodworm obligingly held hands.

ELSA MAXWELL (1883–1963)
American socialite

More than one woman since Lot's wife has betrayed herself by looking back.

AGNES MCPHAIL
(1890–1954)
Canadian suffragette

On being asked by a male heckler whether she didn't wish she were a man

Yes, don't you?

ETHEL MERMAN (1908–1984)
American singer and actress

I can hold a note as long as the Chase National Bank.

On Mary Martin

She's okay if you like talent.

NANCY MITFORD (1904–1973)
British writer

An aristocracy in a republic is like a chicken whose head has been cut off. It may run about in a lovely way, but in fact it's dead.

MARILYN MONROE (1926–1962)
American actress

When they said Canada, I thought it would be up in the mountains somewhere.

On being asked by a journalist whether she didn't have anything on

Yes, I had the radio on.

I've been on a calendar, but never on time.

VIRGINIA OSTMAN

If lawyers are disbarred and clergymen defrocked, doesn't it follow that electricians can be delighted, musicians denoted, cowboys deranged, models deposed, tree surgeons debarked and dry cleaners depressed?

OGDEN NASH (1902–1971)
American poet

On Sally Rand, the fandancer.

Sally Rand
Needs an extra hand.

DOROTHY PARKER (1893–1967)
American writer and wit

Four be the things I'd been better without.
Love, curiosity, freckles and doubt.

> The man she had was kind and clean
> And well enough for every day,
> But oh, dear friends, you should have seen
> The one that got away!

On going into hospital for an abortion

It serves me right for putting all my eggs in one bastard.

On her husband the day their divorce became final

Oh, don't worry about Alan – Alan will always land on somebody's feet.

In a speech to the American Horticultural Society

You can lead a whore to culture but you can't make her think.

He's really awfully fond of coloured people. Well, he says himself, he wouldn't have white servants.

The sweeter the apple, the blacker the core –
Scratch a lover and find a foe!

On Oscar Wilde

If with the literate, I am
Impelled to try an epigram,
I never seek to take the credit;
We all assume that Oscar said it.

In Alexander Woollcott's *While Rome Burns*

If all the young ladies who attended the Yale promenade dance were laid end to end, no one would be the least surprised.

About a starlet leaving a New York restaurant

There goes the good time that's been had by all.

On being asked whether she had enjoyed a cocktail party

Enjoyed it! One more drink and I'd have been under the host.

People Who Do Things exceed my endurance;
God, for a man that solicits insurance!

Three highballs, and I think I'm St Francis of Assisi.

And I'll stay off Verlaine too; he was always chasing Rimbauds.

This is not a novel to be tossed aside lightly. It should be thrown with great force.

Life is a glorious cycle of song
A medley of extemporania
And love is a thing that can never go wrong
And I am Marie of Rumania.

Oh, seek, my love, your newer way;
I'll not be left in sorrow.
So long as I have yesterday,
Go take your damned tomorrow!

On being informed of the death of Calvin Coolidge

How can they tell?

On hearing that Clare Boothe Luce was invariably kind to her inferiors

And where does she find them?

On being told by a fellow guest that their hostess was outspoken

Outspoken! By whom?

Wit has truth in it; wisecracking is simply calisthenics with words.

Ducking for apples – change one letter and it's the story of my life.

On the play *House Beautiful*

House beautiful is play lousy.

Telegram to a friend who had just become a proud mother

Congratulations – we all knew you had it in you.

On being told that a friend had broken a leg while on a visit to London

She probably did it sliding down a barrister.

On her escort refusing to join in a rather childish game, by saying

'I can't. I simply can't bear fools.'

'How odd,' replied Ms Parker. 'Apparently your mother could.'

Brevity is the soul of lingerie.

Guns aren't lawful;
Nooses give;
Gas smells awful;
You might as well live.

The two most beautiful words in the English language are 'Cheque Enclosed'.

Men seldom make passes
At girls who wear glasses.

In her column, *Constant Reader*.
On A. A. Milne's *Winnie the Pooh*

Tonstant Weader fwowed up.

DOLLY PARTON (*b.* 1944)
American singer

I was the first woman to burn my bra – it took the fire department four days to put it out!

VICTORIA PASTERNAK

You'll find in no park or city
A monument to a committee.

IRENE PETER

Always be sincere, even when you don't mean it.

Ms Peter's Law: Today if you're not confused you're just not thinking clearly.

I'm not going to starve to death just so I can live a little longer.

BARONESS PHILLIPS (*b.* 1910)

On the subject of confused people, I liked the store detective who said he'd seen a lot of people so confused that they'd stolen things, but never one so confused that they'd paid twice.

AGNES REPPLIER (1858–1950)
American essayist

Wit is as infinite as love, and a deal more lasting in its qualities.

LILLIAN ROSS

He was almost the only man in Chasen's [restaurant] who was not at that moment looking around at someone other than the person he was talking to.

HELEN ROWLAND (1875–1950)
American journalist

A fool and her money are soon counted.

A bachelor never quite gets over the idea that he is a thing of beauty and a boy for ever.

MARY SCHAFER

They went at it hammer and tongues.

NANCY SPAIN (*d.* 1964)
British journalist

Only a fool would make the bed every day.

MURIEL SPARK (*b.* 1918)
British novelist
In *Voices at Play* ('The Dark Glasses')

But I did not remove my glasses, for I had not asked for her company in the first place, and there is a limit to what one can listen to with the naked eye.

JUDITH STERN

Experience: A comb life gives you after you lose your hair.

MRS ROBERT A. TAFT

I always find that statistics are hard to swallow and impossible to digest. The only one I can ever remember is that if all the people who go to sleep in church were laid end to end they would be a lot more comfortable.

ELIZABETH TAYLOR (*b.* 1932)
British-born actress

A diamond is the only kind of ice that keeps a girl warm.

ANGELA THIRKELL (1890–1961)
British novelist

If one cannot invent a really convincing lie, it is often better to stick to the truth.

IRENE THOMAS (*b.* 1929)
British broadcaster

Protestant women may take the Pill. Roman Catholic women must keep taking the Tablet.

BARBARA WALTERS (*b.* 1931)
American television presenter

Deep breaths are very helpful at shallow parties.

DAME REBECCA WEST (1892–1983)
British novelist

Before a war military science seems a real science, like astronomy. But after a war it seems more like astrology.

MAE WEST (1892–1980)
American film star

It's not the men in my life that counts – it's the life in my men.

You can say what you like about long dresses, but they cover a multitude of shins.

On being asked what she wanted to be remembered for

Everything.

Virtue has its own reward, but no sale at the box office.

When I'm good, I'm very very good, but when I'm bad I'm better.

A curved line is the loveliest distance between two points.

It is better to be looked over than overlooked.

I always say, keep a diary and someday it'll keep you.

A goldrush is what happens when a line of chorus girls spot a man with a bank roll.

On being told that ten men were waiting to meet her at her home

I'm tired, send one of them home.

Between two evils, I always pick the one I never tried before.

On a life-jacket being named after her

I've been in *Who's Who* and I know what's what, but it's the first time I ever made the dictionary.

In her curtain speech after *Catherine was Great*

I'm glad you like my Catherine. I like her too. She ruled thirty million people and had three thousand lovers. I do the best I can in two hours.

It ain't no sin if you crack a few laws now and then, just so long as you don't break any.

I'm a fast-moving girl that likes them slow.

I used to be snow white . . . but I drifted.

I'm never dirty. I'm interesting without being vulgar. I just . . . suggest.

I believe in censorship. After all, I made a fortune out of it. I *invented* censorship.

I'm just a campfire girl.

A man has one hundred dollars and you leave him with two dollars – that's subtraction.

EDITH WHARTON (1862–1937)
American novelist

Blessed are the pure in heart for they have so much more to talk about.

KATHARINE WHITEHORN
British journalist

We were discussing the possibility of making one of our cats Pope recently, and we decided that the fact that she was not Italian, and was female, made the third point, that she was a cat, quite irrelevant.

'How wonderful it must have been for the Ancient Britons,' my mother said once, 'when the Romans arrived and they could have a hot bath.'

I am firm. You are obstinate. He is a pig-headed fool.

Filing is concerned with the past; anything you actually need to see again has to do with the future.

A good listener is not someone who has nothing to say. A good listener is a good talker with a sore throat.

VIRGINIA WOOLF (1882–1941)
British novelist
In *Jacob's Room*

Life would split asunder without letters.

POLITICS

SVETLANA ALLILUYEVA
Daughter of Josef Stalin

I believe in private property.

MARIAN ANDERSON (*b.* 1902)
American singer
On racial prejudice

Sometimes, it's like a hair across your cheek. You can't see it, you can't find it with your fingers, but you keep brushing at it because the feel of it is irritating.

ANONYMOUS REPUBLICAN
On the political philosophy of Tricia Nixon, daughter of Richard Nixon

Slightly to the right of Ivan the Terrible.

SUSAN B. ANTHONY (1820–1906)
American suffragette

Resolved, that the women of this nation in 1876, have greater cause for discontent, rebellion and revolution than the men of 1776.

HANNAH ARENDT (1906–1975)
German-American political philosopher
On violence

If you ask a member of this generation two simple questions: 'How do you want the world to be in fifty years?' and 'What do you want your life to be like five years from now?' the answers are often preceded by 'Provided there is still a world' and 'Provided I am still alive'.

Revolutionaries do not make revolutions. The revolutionaries are those who know when power is lying in the street and then they can pick it up. Armed uprising by itself has never yet led to a revolution.

War has . . . become a luxury which only the small nations can afford.

The Third World is not a reality, but an ideology.

It is far easier to act under conditions of tyranny than to think.

LADY ASTOR (1879–1964)
First woman MP

I am striving to take into public life what any man gets from his mother.

'Sayings of the Week' (*The Observer*, 11 May 1924)

People who talk about peace are very often the most quarrelsome.

The Wait and See Policy has changed me into a fighting woman.

I am a Virginian, so naturally I am a politician.

Nobody wants me as a Cabinet Minister and they are perfectly right. I am an agitator, not an administrator.

VISCOUNT ASTOR (1879–1952)
British politician

When I married Nancy, I hitched my wagon to a star and when I got into the House of Commons in 1910, I found that I had hitched my wagon to a shooting star. In 1919 when she got into the House, I found that I had hitched my wagon to a sort of V-2 rocket.

JOAN BAEZ (*b.* 1941)
American singer

The only thing that's been a worse flop than the organization of non-violence has been the organization of violence.

We're not really pacifists, we're just non-violent soldiers.

Peace might sell, but who's buying?

Music follows a second best when I'm so wrapped up in politics. Half an hour before I go on I get my guitar out of the closet and have to try to remember how to play it.

PEARL BAILEY (*b.* 1918)
American singer

Hungry people cannot be good at learning or producing anything, except perhaps violence.

GERTRUDE BELL (1868–1926)
British traveller, historian, writer
In a letter to her father, 1913

Last night I went to a delightful party at the Glenconners' and just before I arrived (as usual) four suffragettes set on Asquith and seized hold of him. Whereupon Alec Laurence in fury seized two of them and twisted their arms until they shrieked. Then one of them bit him in the hand till he bled. And when he told me the tale he was steeped in his own gore.

RUTH BENEDICT (1887–1948)
American anthropologist

If we justify war it is because all peoples always justify the traits of which they find themselves possessed.

PEG BRACKEN

Why does a slight tax increase cost you two hundred dollars and a substantial tax cut save you thirty cents?

BESSIE BRADDOCK (1899–1970)
British MP

Right now the basic insecurity the workers feel is this: they are haunted by the spectre of the van driving up to the door to take away the TV set.

VERA BRITTAIN (1893–1970)
British writer

Politics are usually the executive expression of human immaturity.

ELAINE BROWN
American radical

Mao Tse-Tung didn't have to deal with people who were watching seven hours of television every day.

PEARL S. BUCK (1892–1973)
American novelist
In *What America Means to Me*

People on the whole are very simple-minded, in whatever country one finds them. They are so simple as to take literally, more often than not, the things their leaders tell them.

None who have always been free can understand the terrible fascinating power of the hope of freedom to those who are not free.

Race prejudice is not only a shadow over the coloured – it is a shadow over all of us, and the shadow is darkest over those who feel it least and allow its evil effects to go on.

RACHEL CARSON (1907–1964)
American scientific writer

Only within the moment of time represented by the present century has one species – man – acquired significant power to alter the nature of his world.

No witchcraft, no enemy action had silenced the rebirth of new life in this stricken world. The people had done it themselves.

SHEILA CASSIDY (*b.* 1936)
British Catholic doctor arrested and tortured in Chile, 1975

The pain was appalling and, determined not to be deceived again, they questioned me with a speed and ferocity that allowed no possibility of fabrication. I don't remember a moment in which I decided to talk . . . Indeed I found it quite impossible to lie for the shocks came with such frequency and intensity that I could no longer think. So, they broke me.

. . . The irony of it was that they found the truth more difficult to believe than the lies I had told them at first and I received many gratuitous shocks because they could not believe the nuns and priests were involved.

SHIRLEY CHISHOLM (*b.* 1924)
American politician

It is a great honour to be chosen as the nation's first black congresswoman. As a United States Representative in Washington, I intend to represent all the people – the blacks, the whites, the men, the women, especially the youth. There are many new ideas abroad in this country and I intend to speak for these ideas. And my voice will be heard.

DIAN COHEN

Having a little inflation is like being a little pregnant; inflation feeds on itself and quickly passes the 'little' mark.

MAUREEN COLQUHOUN (*b.* 1928)
Former British MP

MPs say they can't afford to live on their salaries, but neither can anyone else.

ANGELA DAVIS (*b.* 1944)
American radical

If they come for me in the morning, they will come for you at night.

This culture is one of resistance, but a resistance of desperation.

Living as a fugitive means resisting hysteria, distinguishing between the creations of a frightened imagination and the real signs that the enemy is near.

BERNADETTE DEVLIN (*b.* 1948)
Irish political activist and former MP
After an altercation in the House of Commons

My only regret is that I didn't seize Mr Maudling by the throat.

JOAN DIDION (*b.* 1934)
American writer

To believe in 'the greater good' is to operate, necessarily, in a certain ethical suspension. Ask anyone committed to a Marxist analysis how many angels on the head of a pin, and you will be asked in return to never mind the angels, tell me who controls the production of pins.

ELIZABETH DREW
American journalist

Democracy, like any non-coercive relationship, rests on a shared understanding of limits.

LADY EDEN (*b.* 1920)
Wife of former British Prime Minister, Anthony Eden
On the Suez Crisis, 1956

During the last few weeks I have felt that the Suez Canal was flowing through my drawing-room.

LADY FALKENDER (*b.* 1932)
British political secretary

Once you pass through the door of Number 10 Downing Street, you are in a world that is entirely male-orientated.

ELIZABETH GURLEY FLYN (1890–1965)
American radical

I felt that socialism was just around the corner and I had to get into the struggle as fast as I could.

JANE FONDA (*b.* 1937)
American actress

Bombs are falling on Vietnam, but it is an American tragedy.

To be a revolutionary you have to be a human being. You have to care about people who have no power.

BETTY FORD
Wife of former American President, Gerald Ford

Is there life after the White House?

I don't feel that because I'm First Lady I'm any different from what I was before. It can happen to anyone. After all, it *has* happened to anyone.

How many really intelligent Presidents have we had? I think a President has to be able to think like the people think.

MARY FRANCIS
Wife of crime writer, Dick Francis

You know the phrase 'Black is beautiful' was invented by the whites in South Africa to raise the morale of the black people.

MARGARET FULLER (1810–1850)
American author and critic
In *Summer on the Lakes*

Would that the simple maxim, that honesty is the best policy, might be laid to heart; that a sense of the true aim of life might elevate the tone of politics and trade, and public and private honour become identical.

INDIRA GANDHI (1917–1984)
Indian politician
'Sayings of the Week' (*Observer*, 6 July 1975)

I am proud of democracy in the country and do not want to do anything against it.

You cannot shake hands with a clenched fist.

Politics is the art of acquiring, holding and wielding power.

If you say India has lost her way will you tell me one country which has not?

I would like to ask a question. Would this sort of war or savage bombing which has taken place in Vietnam have been tolerated for so long had the people been European?

MADAME CHARLES DE GAULLE
In Alain de Gaulle's *The Secret Life of My Uncle Charlie*
To her husband

You're running France. I'm running the house.

CHARLES DE GAULLE (1890–1970)
French statesman
On a visit to the USA

If there were anything I could take back to France with me, it would be Mrs Kennedy.

CLAIRE GILLIS

Instead of the government taking over industry when the war broke out, industry took over the government.

HERMIONE GINGOLD (*b.* 1897)
British actress

There are too many men in politics and not enough elsewhere.

EMMA GOLDMAN (1869–1940)
American anarchist

The strongest bulwark of authority is uniformity; the least divergence from it is the greatest crime.

ELLA GRASSO (*b.* 1919)
Governor of Connecticut
On the problems she faced on assuming office, 1975

I bleed a lot. But I try not to leave so much blood all over the floor that I cannot get my work done.

CELIA GREEN
In *The Decline and Fall of Science* ('Aphorisms')

In an autocracy, one person has his way; in an aristocracy, a few people have their way; in a democracy, no one has his way.

MEG GREENFIELD
Quoted in *Newsweek*, 18 December 1978

In government and out, there are vast realms of the bureaucracy dedicated to seeking more information, in perpetuity if need be, in order to avoid taking action.

GERMAINE GREER (*b.* 1939)
Australian feminist
In *The Female Eunuch*

The brotherhood of man will only become a reality, when the consciousness of alien beings corrects man's myopia.

EDITH HAMILTON (1867–1963)
American educator and author

When the freedom they wished for most was freedom from responsibility, then Athens ceased to be free and was never free again.

DENIS HEALEY (*b.* 1917)
British politician

Mrs Thatcher has emerged from the debate as La Passionaria of Privilege . . . She has decided . . . to see her party tagged as the party of the rich few.

LILLIAN HELLMAN (1907–1984)
American playwright

Since when do you have to agree with people to defend them from injustice?

GERTRUDE HIMMELFARB

Liberty too can corrupt, and absolute liberty can corrupt absolutely.

ADA LOUISE HUXTABLE
American writer and critic

Washington is an endless series of mock palaces clearly built for clerks.

DOLORES IBARRURI (*b.* 1895)
Anti-fascist Spanish leader

It is better to die on your feet than to live on your knees.

WASHINGTON IRVING (1783–1859)
In *Knickerbocker's History of New York Book II*

His wife 'ruled the roast', and in governing the governor, governed the province, which might thus be said to be under petticoat government.

LADY BIRD JOHNSON
Wife of former US President, Lyndon Johnson

The First Lady is an unpaid public servant elected by one person – her husband.

BARBARA JORDAN (*b.* 1936)
American politician

If you're going to play the game properly, you'd better know every rule.

Human rights apply equally to Soviet dissidents, Chilean peasants and American women.

I am a politician first, and a black and a woman second and third.

SARA KEAYS (*b.* 1947)
Former mistress of Tory Cabinet minister Cecil Parkinson
On her pregnancy

I was not aware that political expediency was sufficient grounds for an abortion under the 1967 Act.

FLORENCE KENNEDY (*b.* 1916)
American feminist

Oppressed people are frequently very oppressive when first liberated. . . . They know best two positions. Somebody's foot on their neck or their foot on somebody's neck.

JACQUELINE KENNEDY ONASSIS (*b.* 1929)
Wife of 35th US President

You have to have been a Republican to know how good it is to be a Democrat.

There are two kinds of women: those who want power in the world, and those who want power in bed.

JOAN KENNEDY
Former wife of American politician, Edward Kennedy

I've been very close to the presidency. I don't see it as glamorous . . . It's tough. It's risk-taking. It's everything I find unattractive.

ROSE KENNEDY
Mother of John F. Kennedy, Robert F. Kennedy and Edward M. Kennedy

A lot of women have been the mother of one President, but there never has been the mother of two or three Presidents.

GLENYS KINNOCK
Wife of Labour Party leader Neil Kinnock
On her husband's election as leader, 1983

I don't see how Neil will ever be able to help with the shopping again.

MOON LANDRIEU (*b.* 1930)
American politician
On women's role in politics

Women do the lickin' and the stickin'.

SUZANNAH LESSARD
American journalist

The civil servant is not to consider the purpose of what he does; nor even to engage in any activity resembling an expression of political commitment, lest he think about the purposes to which he daily contributes his talents. Awareness of and responsibility for the use of one's work is not only the first principle of integrity, but a basic requisite for a healthy integrated attitude towards what one does with oneself.

LONDONDERRY GIRL
After being tarred and feathered

I'll never go out with a soldier again. If you live in the Bogside you must live by the rules.

CLARE BOOTHE LUCE (*b.* 1903)
American writer and diplomat

The politicians were talking themselves red, white and blue in the face.

ROSA LUXEMBURG (1871–1919)
German revolutionary

Freedom is always and exclusively freedom for the one who thinks differently.

There are only two men left in the party, Klara Zetkin and I.

MARY MCCARTHY (*b.* 1912)
American writer

Congress – these, for the most part, illiterate hacks whose fancy vests are spotted with gravy, and whose speeches, hypocritical, unctuous, and slovenly, are spotted also with the gravy of political patronage.

ANNE O'HARE MCCORMICK (*d.* 1954)
American journalist

Today the real test of power is not capacity to make war but capacity to prevent it.

MARYA MANNES (*b.* 1904)
American novelist and poet

A candidate for office can have no greater advantage than muddled syntax: no greater liability than a command of language.

MARGARET MEAD (1901–1978)
American anthropologist

The United States has the power to destroy the world, but not the power to save it alone.

GOLDA MEIR (1898–1978)
Israeli politician

Don't be humble, you're not that great.

Pessimism is a luxury that a Jew can never allow himself.

We Jews have a secret weapon in our struggle with the Arabs – we have no place to go.

As President Nixon says, presidents can do almost anything, and President Nixon has done many things that nobody would have thought of doing.

I don't want to wake up in the morning and have to worry about how many Arabs were born during the night.

I've never had to kill anyone. I'm not saying it with relief. There's no difference between one's killing and making decisions that will send others to kill.

MARY TYLER MOORE (*b.* 1936)
American actress

There's one beneficial effect of going to Moscow. You come home waving the American flag with all your might!

ELLEN MORPHONIOS
American judge

I have a saying – there's no justice in the law.

ETHEL WATTS MUMFORD (1878–1940)
American writer

Knowledge is power, if you know it about the right person.

FLORENCE NIGHTINGALE (1820–1910)
Nursing pioneer

The War Office is a very slow office, an enormously expensive office, and one in which the Minister's intentions can be entirely negatived by all his sub-departments, and those of each of the sub-departments by every other.

JULIE NIXON
Daughter of impeached former US President, Richard Nixon

It's shattering to be told your father stinks.

CHRISTABEL PANKHURST (1880–1958)
British suffragette

Never lose your temper with the Press or the public is a major rule of political life.

EMMELINE PANKHURST (1857–1928)
British suffragette

The argument of the broken pane of glass is the most valuable argument in modern politics.

ROSA PARKS (*b.* 1913)
Citation, June 1973, at Columbia College, Chicago, awarding an honorary LHD (Rosa Parks had refused to abide by the segregated seating pattern in buses).

Truly when you sat down in a Montgomery, Alabama, bus, all men and women were freed to stand more humanly erect.

ROBERT PATRICK
American playwright
In *Kennedy's Children*

We were marching since we were babies and all we did was make Jane Fonda famous.

EVITA PERON (1919–1952)
Argentine politician

Without fanaticism we cannot accomplish anything.

IRENE PETER

If it were not for space, all matter would be jammed together in one lump and that lump wouldn't take up any room.

SYLVIA PORTER (*b.* 1913)
American economist

One of the soundest rules I try to remember when making forecasts in the field of economics is that whatever is to happen is happening already.

ELEANOR RATHBONE (1872–1946)
British political reformer

A Parliament elected by the universal suffrage of voters grouped according to geographical areas is about as truly representative as a bottle of Bovril is a true representative of an ox.

MADAME ROLAND (1754–1793)
On the French Revolution

O Liberty! O Liberty! What crimes are committed in thy name!

ELEANOR ROOSEVELT (1884–1962)
Wife of 32nd US President

You will feel that you are no longer clothing yourself; you are dressing a public monument.

It is equality of monotony which makes the strength of the British Isles.

THEODORE ROOSEVELT (1858–1919)
26th President of the United States
On Alice Roosevelt, his daughter

I can either try to run the country or try to control Alice. I cannot possibly do both.

RUSSIAN PRESS
Early 1976
On Margaret Thatcher

The Iron Lady.

GEORGE BERNARD SHAW (1856–1950)
Irish playwright
In *Man and Superman*

Give women the vote, and in five years there will be a crushing tax on bachelors.

GRACE SLICK (*b.* 1939)
American rock singer

We thought we could change a mammoth government by wearing flowers and holding hands.

Politics don't provoke many epic rock'n'roll songs today. I can't write about Gerald Ford bumping his head.

I was appalled when the San Francisco ethic didn't mushroom and envelope the whole world into this loving community of acid freaks. I was very naïve.

MARGARET CHASE SMITH (*b.* 1897)
American politician

Before you can become a statesman you first have to get elected. And to get elected you have to be a politician, pledging support for what the voters want.

SUSAN SONTAG (*b.* 1933)
American essayist

The white race is the cancer of history.

MADAME DE STAËL (1766–1817)
French writer

A nation has character only when it is free.

GLORIA STEINEM (*b.* 1934)
American feminist

Intelligence at the service of poor instinct is really dangerous.

America is an enormous frosted cupcake in the middle of millions of starving people.

BARONESS MARY STOCKS (1891–1975)
British politician

The House of Lords is a perfect eventide home.

MARGARET THATCHER (*b.* 1925)
British politician

Most of us have stopped using silver every day.

I've a woman's ability to stick to a job and get on with it when everyone else walks off and leaves it.

I hope to be Prime Minister one day and I do not want there to be one street in Britain I cannot go down.

Perhaps this country needs an Iron Lady.

If unions hold the whip hand, upon whose backs does the lash fall?

You may have to fight a battle more than once to win it.

It is not the business of politicians to please everyone.

If someone is confronting our essential liberties, if someone is inflicting injury and harm – by God, I'll confront them.

In *Sunday Telegraph*, 26 October 1969

No woman in my time will be Prime Minister or Chancellor or Foreign Secretary – not the top jobs. Anyway, I wouldn't want to be Prime Minister, you have to give yourself 100 per cent.

You don't tell deliberate lies; but sometimes you have to be evasive.

The Prime Minister is stealing our clothes . . . but he's going to look pretty ridiculous walking around in mine.

Fear is no basis for foreign policy.

No one would remember the Good Samaritan if he only had good intentions. He had money as well.

Never in the history of human credit has so much been owed.

The lady's not for turning.

I just can't stand hot air.

I will continue to be the essence of sweet reasonableness.

MARGARET TRUDEAU (*b.* 1948)
Former wife of Canadian Prime Minister
'Sayings of the Week' (*The Observer*, 8 April 1979)

I wrote out a little list of questions for Pierre to put to the Pope about our marriage problems.

BARBARA TUCHMAN (*b.* 1912)
American historian
In *The Guns of August*

No more distressing moment can ever face a British government than that which requires it to come to a hard and fast and specific decision.

Dead battles, like dead generals, hold the military mind in their dead grip.

War is the unfolding of miscalculations.

Tuchman's Law: If power corrupts, weakness is the seat of power, with its constant necessity of deals and bribes and comprising arrangements, corrupts even more.

On the 1980 Presidential candidates

God! The country that produced George Washington has got this collection of crumb-bums!

Every successful revolution puts on in time the robes of the tyrant it has deposed.

SIMONE WEIL (1909–1943)
French philosopher

Liberty, taking the word in its concrete sense, consists in the ability to choose.

What a country calls its vital economic interests are not the things which enable its citizens to live, but the things which enable it to make war. Petrol is more likely than wheat to be a cause of international conflict.

KATHARINE WHITEHORN
British journalist

It is a pity, as my husband says, that more politicians are not bastards by birth instead of vocation.

ELLEN WILKINSON (1891–1947)
British politician

In 1930

It is eleven years since Lady Astor put English women in her debt by standing her ground in a parliament 'of men who looked as if they had done well in the war', as she put it. If she cannot get what she wants by logical argument, then she tosses that overboard and gets there anyway.

TOYAH WILLCOX (*b.* 1958)
British actress and singer

If this world has a revolution I know I'll really enjoy myself.

SHIRLEY WILLIAMS (*b.* 1930)
British politician, co-founder of the SDP

The saddest illusion of revolutionary socialists is that revolution itself will transform the nature of human beings.

There are hazards in anything one does, but there are greater hazards in doing nothing.

Comprehensive schools demonstrate that we are all members of one family, of one society.

25 May 1980

I am not interested in a third party. I do not believe that it has any future.

THE WOMEN'S MOVEMENT

SUSANNA AGNELLI

Men do consider that their penis is a fantastic object.

ANONYMOUS FEMINIST

At the time of the 1979 General Election

Mrs Thatcher may be a woman, but she isn't a sister.

SUSAN B. ANTHONY (1820–1906)

American suffragette

The only question left to be settled now is, are women persons?

In a letter to Elizabeth C. Stanton, June 1856

Will you load my gun, leaving me only to pull the trigger and let fly the powder and ball?

On Mrs Stanton having addressed a convention on the subject of divorce, 1860

As usual when she had fired her gun she went home and left me to finish the battle.

PEARL BAILEY (*b.* 1918)

American singer

Someone asked me . . . whether I 'marched'. I said, 'No. I haven't marched any place physically, but I march every day in my heart. I live with humanity every day, and when you live with humanity then you have walked – and the road is not easy necessarily.'

BRIGITTE BARDOT (*b.* 1933)

French actress

Women get more unhappy the more they try to liberate themselves.

SIMONE DE BEAUVOIR (*b.* 1908)
French writer

No one is born a woman.

Woman is not completed reality, but rather a becoming.

When an individual is kept in a situation of inferiority, the fact is that he does become inferior.

NAN BERGER and JOAN MAIZELS
British journalists
In *Woman Fancy or Free?*

Differential treatment breeds the illusion that girls will grow up to spend their lives looking after children who will never grow up and a family which remains always dependent. But the family is composed of children who in the process of their growth become increasingly self-reliant and of mature men who are, it is assumed, already so. It is inconsistent to plan women's education on the assumption that they will be exclusively tied to their families for the whole of their lives when the facts contradict this fantasy.

AMELIA BLOOMER (1818–1894)
American feminist

In the minds of some people the short dress and women's rights were inseparably connected. With us, the dress was but an incident, and we were not willing to sacrifice greater questions to it.

CARYL BRAHMS (*c.* 1900–1983)
and S. J. SIMON
British writing team
In *No Nightingales*

The suffragettes were triumphant. Woman's place was in the gaol.

SUSAN BROWNMILLER (*b.* 1933)
American feminist

Rape is a dull, blunt, ugly act committed by punk kids, their cousins and older brothers, not by charming, witty, unscrupulous, heroic, sensual rakes, or by timid souls deprived of a 'normal' sexual outlet, or by *supermenschen* possessed of uncontrollable lust.

ANITA BRYANT (*b.* 1940)
American anti-homosexual campaigner

As a mother, I know that homosexuals cannot biologically reproducc children; therefore, they must recruit our children.

I love gay people . . . But they are not a minority whose rights have to be protected. They are not like blacks, because black sticks . . . If gays are granted rights, next we'll have to give rights to prostitutes, and to people who sleep with Saint Bernards and to nail-biters.

SHIRLEY CHISHOLM (*b.* 1924)
American politician

Women must become revolutionary. This cannot be evolution but revolution.

The emotional, sexual, and psychological stereotyping of females begins when the doctor says, 'It's a girl'.

JACKIE COLLINS
British writer

So many men find it hard to react if a girl says to them at a party: 'What's your telephone number? I'll call you tomorrow.'

FLORA DRUMMOND
British suffragette
On Christabel Pankhurst

She knows everything and can see through everything.

FAYE DUNAWAY (*b.* 1941)
American actress

I'm all for women's lib, but does the price of freedom have to be unemployment?

NORA EPHRON (*b.* 1941)
American journalist

We have lived through the era when happiness was a warm puppy, and the era when happiness was a dry Martini, and now we have come to the era when happiness is 'knowing what your uterus looks like'.

One of the trump cards that men who are threatened by women's liberation are always dredging up is the question of whether there is sex after liberation.

DAME MILLICENT FAWCETT (1849–1929)
British suffragette

I can never feel that setting fire to houses and churches and letter-boxes and destroying valuable pictures really helps to convince people that women ought to be enfranchised.

BETTY FRIEDAN (*b.* 1921)
American feminist
In *The Feminine Mystique*

A mystique does not compel its own acceptance.

The feminine mystique has succeeded in burying millions of American women alive.

It is easier to live through someone else than to become complete yourself.

Who knows what women can be when they are finally free to become themselves?

Man is not the enemy here, but the fellow victim. The real enemy is women's denigration of themselves.

PROFESSOR HANS FRIEDENTHAL
On 'the new woman', 1914

Brainwork will cause her to become bald, while increasing masculinity and contempt for beauty will induce the growth of hair on the face. In the future, therefore, women will be bald and will wear long moustaches and patriarchal beards.

GERMAINE GREER (*b.* 1939)
Australian feminist

Most women still need a room of their own and the only way to find it may be outside their own homes.

Freud is the father of psychoanalysis. It has no mother.

Revolution is the festival of the oppressed.

The stereotype is the Eternal Feminine. She is the Sexual Object sought by all men, and by all women. She is of neither sex, for she herself has no sex at all.

Probably the only place where a man can feel really secure is in a maximum security prison, except for the imminent threat of release.

Quoted in *Playboy*, 1972

Pigs may like honey, but that doesn't stop it being sweet.

We've been castrated. It's all very well to let a bullock out into the field when you've already cut off his balls because he's not going to do anything. That's exactly what's happened to women.

In *The Female Eunuch*

The consequences of militancy do not disappear when the need for militancy is over.

Reviews of *The Female Eunuch*

A detailed exposition, of chilling clarity, that guarantees a cosmic persecution complex to any woman reading it. Jill Tweedie, *Guardian*

This good lady . . . seeks to prove that there is no good biological reason why women shouldn't run the world. *Good Housekeeping*

A manual of self-help for women-kind. How to learn to stop nagging, crabbing and grabbing and make your own life. *Evening Standard*

Passionate and personal and likely to set fastidious teeth on edge. *The Times*

Lively, aggressive . . . knowledgeable, intelligent and

witty . . . she talks very good sense. Claire Tomalin, *New Statesman*

CAROLYN G. HEILBRUN

Today's youth seem finally to have understood that only by freeing woman from her exclusively sexual role can man free himself from his ordained role in the rat-race; that of the rat.

ABBIE HOFFMAN (*b.* 1936)
American radical

The only alliance I would make with the Women's Liberation Movement is in bed.

SHERE HITE
American writer and sexologist

We have a right to our own bodies.

You cannot decree women to be sexually free when they are not economically free.

All too many men still seem to believe, in a rather naïve and egocentric way, that what feels good to them is automatically what feels good to women.

GEMMA HUSSEY
Irish senator

The Government is making the dangerous assumption that the head of a household is always a man.

BARBARA JORDAN (*b.* 1936)
American politician

As I would not be a slave, so I would not be a master. Whatever differs from this, to the extent of the difference, is no democracy.

CAROL KLEIMAN
Quoted in *Ms*, April 1978

Not only am I angry, but I'm also angry at all the years I wasn't angry.

EMMELINE PETHWICK-LAWRENCE (1867–1954)
British suffragette
On Christabel Pankhurst

Christabel cared less for the political vote itself than for the dignity of her sex, and she denounced the false dignity earned by submission and extolled the true dignity accorded by revolt. . . . Militancy to her meant the putting off of the slave *spirit*.

HELEN LAWRENSON
American journalist

You have to go back to the Children's Crusade in 1212 AD to find as unfortunate and fatuous an attempt at manipulated hysteria as the Women's Liberation Movement.

ANITA LOOS (*b.* 1893)
American novelist

The people I'm furious with are the women's liberationists. They keep getting up on soapboxes and proclaiming women are brighter than men. That's true, but it should be kept quiet or it ruins the whole racket.

GOLDA MEIR (1898–1978)
Israeli politician

Whether women are better than men I cannot say – but I can say they are certainly no worse.

Women's liberation is just a lot of foolishness. It's the men who are discriminated against. They can't bear children. And no one's likely to do anything about that.

How does it feel to be a woman minister? I don't know; I've never been a man minister.

In *My Life*
On her inattention to her children

You can get used to anything if you have to, even to feeling perpetually guilty.

BOB MELVIN

The women's movement . . . would probably run more smoothly if men were running it.

KATE MILLETT (*b.* 1934)
American feminist

Isn't privacy about keeping taboos in their place?

The image of woman as we know it is an image created by men and fashioned to suit their needs.

Male supremacy, like other political creeds, does not finally reside in physical strength but in acceptance of a value system which is not biological.

In *Sexual Politics*

Literary criticism of the Brontës has been a long game of masculine prejudice wherein the player either proves they can't write and are hopeless primitives, whereupon the critic sets himself up like a schoolmaster to edit their stuff and point out where they went wrong, or converts them into case histories from the wilds . . .

On Ayatolla Khomeini

Male chauvinist is a simple, idiotic way of describing him.

MARTHA MITCHELL
Former wife of American politician

I'm the most liberated woman in the world. Any woman can be liberated if she wants to be. First, she has to convince her husband.

MARIANNE MOORE (1887–1972)
American poet

Impatience is the mark of independence, not of bondage.

ROBIN MORGAN (*b.* 1941)
American feminist

Women are not inherently passive or peaceful. We're not inherently anything but human.

ALVA MYRDAL and VIOLA KLEIN
American writers
In *Women's Two Roles*

The sentimental cult of domestic virtues is the cheapest method at society's disposal of keeping women quiet without seriously considering their grievances or improving their position.

LINDA NOCHLIN
In Vivian Gornick and Barbara K. Moran's *Woman in Sexist Society*

Ovbiously, for wolves, be they in sheep's clothing or in mufti, it is always best to refer to the lamb problem in the interests of public relations, as well as for the good of the lupine conscience.

KATHLEEN NORRIS (1900–1966)
American novelist

There are men I could spend eternity with,
But not this life.

FRANK O'CONNOR (1903–1966)
Irish novelist and playwright

No man is an anti-feminist as a really feminine woman.

EMMELINE PANKHURST (1857–1928)
British suffragette

There is something that governments care for far more than human life, and that is the security of property, and so it is through property that we shall strike the enemy . . . I incite this meeting to rebellion.

I was a Poor Law Guardian, and it was my duty to go through a workhouse infirmary, and I shall never forget seeing a little girl of thirteen lying on a bed playing with a doll. I was told she was on the eve of becoming a mother, and she was infected with a loathsome disease, and on the point of bringing, no doubt, a diseased child into the world . . . We women suffragists have a great mission – the greatest mission the world has ever known. It is to free half the human race, and through that freedom to save the rest.

LAURENCE J. PETER (*b.* 1919)
Canadian academic

Most hierarchies were established by men who now monopolise the upper levels, thus depriving women of their rightful share of opportunities to achieve incompetence.

LETTY COTTIN POGREBIN (*b.* 1939)
American writer

No labourer in the world is expected to work for room, board and love – except the housewife.

We are refusing to be trivialised.

MARIO PUZO (*b.* 1920)
American novelist
In *Fools Die*

The women's liberation warriors think they have something new, but it's just their armies coming out of the guerrilla hills. Sweet women ambushed men always: at their cradles, in the kitchen, the bedroom . . .

ADRIENNE RICH (*b.* 1929)
American feminist

All human life on the planet is born of woman.

In *On Lies, Secrets and Silence*

I believe that a militant and pluralistic lesbian/feminist movement is potentially the greatest force in the world today for a complete transformation of society and of our relation to all life. It goes far beyond any struggle for civil liberties or equal rights – necessary as those struggles continue to be. In its deepest, most inclusive form it is an inevitable process by which women will claim our primary and central vision in shaping the future.

Feminism begins but cannot end with the discovery by an individual of her self-consciousness as a woman. It is not, finally, even the recognition of her reasons for anger . . . Feminism means finally that we renounce our obedience to the fathers and recognise that the world they have described is not the whole world.

BOBBY RIGGS
American tennis player
About to play against Billie Jean King, 20 September 1973

She's a great player for a gal. But no woman can beat a male player who knows what he's doing. I'm not only interested in glory for my own sex, but I also want to set women's lib back twenty years, to get women back into the home, where they belong.

(Billie Jean won the match in straight sets, 6–4, 6–3, 6–3)

BETTY ROLLIN
American feminist

Women have child-bearing equipment. For them to choose not to use the equipment is no more blocking what is instinctive than it is for a man who, muscles or no, chooses not to be a weight-lifter.

Scratch most feminists and underneath there is a woman who longs to be a sex object. The difference is that is not *all* she longs to be.

JILL RUCKELSHAUS
American feminist

No one should have to dance backward all their lives.

MARGARET SANGER (1883–1966)
American leader of birth control movement

No woman can call herself free who does not own and control her body. No woman can call herself free until she can choose consciously whether she will or will not be a mother.

PHYLLIS SCHLAFFY (*b.* 1924)

We cannot reduce women to equality. Equality is a step down for most women.

LAURA SHAPIRO
Quoted in *Ms*, April 1978

Watch out for men who have mothers.

DR MARY JANE SHERFEY
In *Nature and Evolution of Female Sexuality*

Embryologically speaking, it is correct to say that the penis is an exaggerated clitoris.

GRACE SLICK (*b.* 1939)
American rock singer

I never had to become a feminist; I was born liberated.

ARIANNA STASSINOPOULOS (*b.* 1950)
Greek writer

Emancipation means equal status for different roles.

GLORIA STEINEM (*b.* 1934)
American feminist

The first problem for all of us, men and women, is not to learn, but to unlearn.

A woman without a man is like a fish without a bicycle.

Once upon a time . . . a Liberated Woman was someone who had sex before marriage and a job afterward.

A woman cab driver to Gloria Steinem, Boston, 1971

'If men could get pregnant, abortion would be a sacrament.'

We are talking about overthrowing, or humanising – pick your verb, depending how patient you feel – the sex and race cast systems. Now that is a big job.

MARGARET THATCHER (*b.* 1925)
British politician

I owe nothing to Women's Lib.

LILY TOMLIN (*b.* 1939)
American comedienne

We're all in this together – by ourselves.

MAO TSE-TUNG (1893–1976)
Chinese statesman

Men and women must receive equal pay for equal work in production. Genuine equality between sexes can only be realised in the process of the socialist transformation of society as a whole.

SOJOURNER TRUTH (1797–1883)
American abolitionist, born a slave

Where did your Christ come from? From God and a woman! Man had nothing to do with him.

QUEEN VICTORIA (1819–1901)
To Sir Theodore Martin, 29 May 1870

The Queen is most anxious to enlist everyone who can speak or write to join in checking this mad, wicked folly of 'Woman's Rights' with all its attendant horrors on which her poor, feeble sex is bent, forgetting every sense of womanly feeling and propriety. Lady . . . ought to get a whipping. It is a subject which makes the Queen so furious that she cannot contain herself.

BARBARA WARD (1914–1981)
British economist

I have the impression that when we talk so confidently of liberty, we are unaware of the awful servitude, of poverty when means are so small that there is literally no choice.

SEXISM

MARCEL ACHARD (*b.* 1900)
French playwright

Women like silent men. They think they're listening.

ANONYMOUS

There is one woman whom fate has destined for each of us. If we miss her, we are saved.

MATTHEW ARNOLD (1822–1888)
British poet

With women, the heart argues, not the mind.

ANTONIN ARTAUD (1896–1948)
French playwright

Evil comes from the darkness of women.

WARREN BEATTY (*b.* 1937)
American actor

Women are a problem, but if you haven't already guessed, they're the kind of problem I enjoy wrestling with.

WILLIAM BAYER

The only area where women have achieved equal status is in the profession of acting, and that is because *there* they are a necessity.

SIR THOMAS BEECHAM (1897–1961)
British conductor

There are no women composers, never have been and possibly never will be.

The trouble with women in an orchestra is that if they are attractive it will upset my players and if they're not it will upset me.

On asking a soprano how she was getting on with learning the oratorio in Handel's *Messiah*.

'I've been working hard on it,' she replied. 'The score goes with me everywhere – to work, to meals, up to bed at night . . .'

'Then,' he replied, 'may I trust we may look forward to an immaculate conception?'

Criticising the dying Mimi, in the rehearsal of the last act of *La Bohème*, for not being able to make herself heard

When the lady protested that one couldn't give of one's best when in the prone position.

'I seem to recollect,' he replied, 'that I have given some of my best performances in that position.'

MAX BEERBOHM (1872–1956)
British writer and caricaturist

Most women are not so young as they are painted.

PRINCE BERNHARD
Consort of Queen Juliana of the Netherlands

Mummy is the head of state, and I am boss in the house.

THE BIBLE
Genesis 3:16

To the woman He said, 'I will greatly multiply your pain in child bearing; in pain you shall bring forth children yet your desire shall be for your husband and he shall rule over you.'

JACQUES BOSSUET (1627–1704)
French writer

The cruelest revenge of a woman is to stay faithful to a man.

ANATOLE BROYARD

For years they have been using the role of 'sex object' as a cover while they spied out the land.

JEAN DE LA BRUYÈRE (1645–1696)
French writer

Women become attached to men by the favours they grant them: men are cured by these same favours.

ARCHIE BUNKER
Fictional American television character

All right, Edith, you go right ahead and do your thing . . . but just remember that your thing is eggs over-easy and crisp bacon.

The only thing that holds a marriage together is the husband bein' big enough to step back and see where his wife is wrong.

EDMUND BURKE (1729–1797)
British statesman and philosopher

A woman is but an animal, and an animal not of the highest order.

ROBERT BURTON (1577–1640)
British writer

An eminent philosopher insists that no woman should come abroad more than three times in her whole life: first, to be baptised; then to be married; and, lastly, to be entombed. Extravagant, however, as this idea is, and different as a prison is from privacy, it may be fairly supposed to intimate, that the highest honour of a virtuous female, is a rational seclusion and retreat.

SAMUEL BUTLER (1612–1680)
British writer

The souls of women are so small
That some believe they've none at all.

Brigands demand your money or your life; women require both.

JULIUS CAESAR (100 or 102–44 BC)
Roman general and statesman

Caesar's wife must be above suspicion.

PIERRE CARDIN (*b.* 1922)
French couturier

For a woman to be loved, she usually ought to be naked.

THOMAS CARLYLE (1795–1881)
British historian
On George Eliot's *Adam Bede*

I found out in the first two pages that it was a woman's writing – she supposed that in making a door, you last of all put in the *panels*!

STOKELY CARMICHAEL (*b.* 1941)
American radical

The only position for women in SNCC is prone.

DE CASSERES

Can you recall a woman who ever showed you with pride her library?

JOSEPH CHAMBERLAIN (1836–1914)
British statesman
In a letter to Lord Milner, 25 January 1901
On Queen Victoria

She was the greatest of Englishwomen – I had almost said of Englishmen – for she added the highest of manly qualities to the personal delicacy of the woman.

CHARLIE CHAN
Fictional Chinese detective

Good wife best household furniture.

MALCOLM DE CHAZAL

Adultery is a stimulant to men but a sedative to women.

EARL OF CHESTERFIELD (1694–1773)
British statesman and letter-writer
In letters to his son

Women, then, are only children of a larger growth; they have an entertaining tattle, and sometimes wit; but for solid, reasoning good sense, I never knew in my life one that had it, or who reasoned or acted consequentially for four and twenty hours together.

Women are much more like each other than men; they have in truth, but two passions, vanity and love; these are their universal characteristics.

A man of sense only trifles with them, plays with them, humours and flatters them, as he does with a sprightly and forward child; but he neither consults them about, nor trusts them with, serious matters.

GROVER CLEVELAND (1837–1908)
22nd and 24th President of the United States

Sensible and responsible women do not want to vote. The relative positions to be assumed by man and woman in the working out of our civilisation were assigned long ago by a higher intelligence than ours.

CONFUCIAN MARRIAGE MANUAL

The five worst infirmities that afflict the female are indocility, discontent, slander, jealousy and silliness.

BERNARD CORNFELD
British businessman

A beautiful woman with a brain is like a beautiful woman with a club foot.

GEORGE CRABBE (1754–1832)
English poet

The wife was pretty, trifling, childish, weak;
She could not think, but would not cease to speak.

JACQUES DEVAL

Women never use their intelligence – except when they need to prop up their intuition.

BENJAMIN DISRAELI (1804–1881)
British statesman and author
In *Lothair*

Every woman should marry – and no man.

On his wife

She is an excellent creature, but she never can remember which came first, the Greeks or the Romans.

ALEXANDRE DUMAS (1802–1870)
French novelist and playwright

Woman inspires us to great things, and prevents us from achieving them.

DWIGHT D. EISENHOWER (1890–1969)
Former American President

Well, it's hard for a mere man to believe that a woman doesn't have equal rights.

DR ALBERT ELLIS (*b.* 1913)
American psychologist

For a man there are three certainties in life: death, taxes, and women. It is often difficult to say which is the worst.

EURIPIDES (484–406 BC)
Greek playwright

Neither earth nor ocean produces a creature as savage and monstrous as woman.

DOUG FIEGER
Rock singer (*The Knack*)

Girls come to our shows because they want to go to bed with us without any fear that afterwards they're going to be thought of as sluts and whores. They're pure, pretty, beautiful, and so very horny.

JOHN FISKE (1842–1901)
American historian
In a letter to his wife, 1873
On George Eliot

I never saw such a woman. There is nothing a bit masculine about her; she is thoroughly feminine and looks and acts as if she were made for nothing but to mother babies.

EDWARD FITZGERALD (1809–1883)
British writer and translator
On the death of Elizabeth Barrett Browning

Mrs Browning's death was rather a relief to me
I must say; no more *Aurora Leighs*, thank God.

ROBERT FROST (1874–1963)
American poet

A mother takes twenty years to make a man of her boy and another woman makes a fool of him in twenty minutes.

There is one thing more exasperating than a wife who can cook and won't, and that's the wife who can't cook and will!

EMILE GABORIAU (1835–1873)
French writer of detective novels

A woman scoffs at evidence. Show her the sun, tell her it is daylight, at once she will close her eyes and say to you, 'No, it is night.'

JACK GELBER (*b.* 1932)
American writer

Give a woman a job and she grows balls.

W. S. GILBERT (1836–1911)
British librettist and parodist

In all the woes that curse our race
There is a lady in the case.

JEAN GIRADOUX (1882–1944)
French writer

A pretty woman has the right to be ignorant of everything provided she knows when to keep still.

GEORGE GOODMAN ('Adam Smith')
In *The Money Game*

A crowd has the mind of a woman.

GEORGE GRANVILLE (1815–1891)
British statesman

Of all the plagues with which the world is cursed,
Of every ill, a woman is the worst.

In *The British Enchanters*

Who to a woman trusts his peace of mind,
Trusts a frail bark, with a tempestuous wind.

In *The Vision*

Whimsy, not reason, is the female guide.

WILLIAM HAZLITT (1778–1830)
British critic and essayist

Women never reason, and therefore they are (comparatively) seldom wrong.

SIR SEYMOUR HICKS (1871–1949)
British actor-manager

A man does not buy his wife a fur coat to keep her warm, but to keep her pleasant.

JOHN HOME (1722–1808)

He seldom errs
Who thinks the worst he can of womankind.

EDGAR WATSON HOWE (1853–1937)

A woman does not spend all her time in buying things; she spends part of it in taking them back.

L. RON HUBBARD
Founder of Scientology

A society in which women are taught anything but the management of a family, the care of men, and the creation of the future generation is a society which is on the way out.

DR SAMUEL JOHNSON (1709–1784)
British writer

Nature has given women so much power that the law has very wisely given them little.

Sir, a woman preaching is like a dog's walking on his hind legs. It is not done well; but you are surprised to find it done at all.

As the faculty of writing has been chiefly a masculine endowment, the reproach of making the world miserable has been always thrown upon the women.

On the remarriage of a widower

Alas! Another instance of the triumph of hope over experience.

On Diana Beauclerk

The woman's a whore, and there's an end on't.

On being accused by a lady that he seemed to prefer the company of men to that of ladies

'Madam, you are mistaken. I am very fond of the company of ladies. I like their beauty, I like their vivacity, and I like their silence.'

KAISER NEWS
No. 5, 1971

The automobile is the woman in technological man's life; his mistress, wife and mother.

TAIJI KAWATE
Japanese broadcasting executive

I fired my female employees because they weren't beautiful any more.

JOHN KEATS (1795–1821)
British poet

Woman! when I behold thee flippant, vain,
Inconstant, childish, proud, and full of fancies.

RUDYARD KIPLING (1865–1936)
British writer
In *The Betrothed*

And a woman is only a woman, but a good cigar is a smoke.

JOHN KNOX (1505–1575)
Scottish reformer
In *The First Blast of the Trumpet Against the Monstrous Regiment of Women*

Nature, I say, doth paynt them further to be weak, fraile, impacient, feble and foolishe; and experience hath declared them to be unconstant, variable, cruell, and lacking the spirit of counsel and regiment.

BILL LAWRENCE
American newsman
To J. F. Kennedy
On admitting women to the all-male Gridiron Club

Look, Mr President, I might sleep with them, but I'm damned if I'll eat lunch with them.

LORD JUSTICE LAWTON (*b.* 1911)
British lawyer

Wife beating may be socially acceptable in Sheffield, but it is a different matter in Cheltenham.

GEORG CHRISTOPH LICHTENBERG (1764–1799)
German physicist

Nowadays beautiful women are counted among the talents of their husbands.

MARTIN LUTHER (1483–1546)
German religious reformer

Women should remain at home, sit still, keep house, and bear and bring up children.

GEORGE (Baron) LYTTELTON (1709–1773)
In *Advice to a Lady*

Seek to be good, but aim not to be great;
A woman's noblest station is retreat.

W. SOMERSET MAUGHAM (1874–1965)
British writer
In *The Circle*

A woman will always sacrifice herself if you give her the opportunity. It is her favourite form of self-indulgence.

JOHN MILTON (1608–1674)
British writer
In *Paradise Lost*

Nothing lovelier can be found
In woman, than to study household good,
And good works in her husband to promote.

MOHAMMED (570–632)
Prophet

Verily the best of women are those who are content with little.

MAFIA MOTTO

Never loan shylock money to a woman, because you can't beat her up to collect.

ROBERT MUELLER

I asked a Burmese why women, after centuries of following their men, now walk in front. He said there were many unexploded land mines since the war.

OGDEN NASH (1902–1971)
American poet
In *Frailty, Thy Name is a Misnomer*

Women would rather be right than reasonable.

FRIEDRICH WILHELM NIETZSCHE (1844–1900)
German philosopher

Woman learns how to hate in the degree that she forgets how to charm.

Where neither love nor hatred is in the game, a woman's game is mediocre.

The happiness of man is: I will. The happiness of woman is: he wills.

Let man fear woman when she loves: then she makes any sacrifice, and everything else seems without value to her.

TED NUGENT (*b.* 1949)
American punk rock singer

There's nothing I like better than making love to a chick with a gun, know what I mean? I've got a girlfriend who's a cop back in Michigan and I go nuts when she keeps her holster on.

JACK PARR (*b.* 1918)
American television performer

I'm just naturally respectful of pretty girls in tight-fitting sweaters.

MR JUSTICE PAYNE
(*Observer*, 27 May 1979)

A man ought not to give up work and turn himself into a mother figure.

SAMUEL PEPYS (1633–1703)
British diarist
In his *Diary*, 25 December 1665

Strange to say what delight we married people have to see these poor fools decoyed into our condition.

PETRONIUS (1st century AD)
Roman writer

Women are one and all a set of vultures.

PABLO PICASSO (1881–1973)
Spanish painter

There are only two kinds of women – goddesses and doormats.

There's nothing so similar to one poodle dog as another poodle dog and that goes for women, too.

The best prescription for a discontented female is to have a child.

PLAUTUS (250–184 BC)
Roman playwright

There's no such thing, you know, as picking out the best woman: it's only a question of comparative badness, brother.

ALEXANDER POPE (1688–1744)
English poet

Most women have no characters at all.

Men, some to business, some to pleasure take
But every woman is at heart a rake.

PLUTARCH (*c.* AD 46–120)
Greek biographer

When the candles are out, all women are fair.

JEAN RACINE (1639–1699)
French dramatist

She wavers, she hesitates; in one word, she is a woman.

SALLY RAND (1904–1979)
American fan-dancer

I never made any money till I took off my pants.

THEODORE REIK (1888–1969)
American psychologist
In *Of Love and Lust*

Women see through each other, but they rarely look into themselves.

In *New York Times*, 1 January 1970

I have come across some women in analytic practice who lacked the faculty of being catty. They were either emotionally perverted, masochistic, homosexual, or neurotic.

PIERRE AUGUSTE RENOIR (1841–1919)
French Impressionist artist

I consider that women who are authors, lawyers and politicians are monsters.

FRANK RICHARDSON

I'm not a woman-hater. Life is only long enough to allow even an energetic man to hate one woman – adequately.

BOBBY RIGGS
American tennis player

A woman's place is in the bedroom and the kitchen, in that order.

MORT SAHL (*b.* 1926)
American comedian

In the forties, to get a girl you had to be a GI or a jock. In the fifties, to get a girl you had to be Jewish. In the sixties, to get a girl you had to be black. In the seventies, to get a girl you've got to be a girl.

RAT SCABIES (Chris Miller)
British punk rock singer (*The Damned*)

I have a great interest in rolling on PVC sheets, smothered in olive oil, with 16-year-old skinny boilers.

ARTUR SCHOPENHAUER (1788–1860)
German philosopher

The fundamental fault of the female character is that it has no sense of justice.

In their hearts women think that it is men's business to earn money and theirs to spend it.

SPANISH PROVERBS

Women, melons, and cheese should be chosen by weight.

Women and calendars are good only for a year.

JOHN STEINBECK (1903–1968)
American novelist

The American girl makes a servant of her husband and then finds him contemptible for being a servant.

CAT STEVENS (*b.* 1947)
British rock singer

I'm constantly falling asleep on them. I've never felt satisfied. Ever.

ALLEN D. THOMAS

Women add zest to the unlicensed hours.

JAMES THURBER (1894–1961)
American writer

A woman's place is in the wrong.

PAUL VALÉRY (1871–1945)
French writer and poet
God created man and, finding him not sufficiently alone, gave him a companion to make him feel his solitude more keenly.

JOHN WAYNE (1907–1980)
American actor

They have a right to work wherever they want to – as long as they have dinner ready when you get home.

H. G. WELLS (1866–1946)
British novelist and sociologist
In a letter to his wife, quoted in Gordon N. Ray's *H. G. Wells and Rebecca West*

I want a healthy woman handy to steady my nerves and leave my mind free for real things.

OSCAR WILDE (1854–1900)
British writer

Dear . . . she is one of nature's gentlemen.

In *The Importance of Being Earnest*
The only way to behave to a woman is to make love to her, if she is pretty, and to someone else if she is plain.

THORNTON WILDER (*b.* 1897)
American playwright
In *The Matchmaker*

There's nothing like mixing with woman to bring out all the foolishness in a man of sense.

DR J. ROBERT WILLSON
In *Obstetrics and Gynaecology*

The traits that compose the core of the female personality are feminine narcissism, masochism and passivity.

GRAFFITI

Jesus was a typical man – they always say they'll come back but you never see them again

Every time I see him my knees turn to jelly. Is it love or is it fear?

Porn is the theory. Rape is the practice

Feel superior – become a nun

A girl of 17 is much more of a woman than a boy of 17

If the cap fits wear it

A woman's work is never done by men!

Every mother is a working mother

Wicked witches were invented by frightened men

When God created man she was only experimenting

A woman without a man is like a neck without a pain

Marriage is a bed of roses. Look out for the thorns

Better to have loved and lost than to have spent your whole damn life with him

All relationships are give and take – you give, he takes

A little yearning is a dangerous thing

Behind every great woman there's a man who tried to stop her

Don't accept rides from strange men and remember – *all* men are strange as hell

My mother made me a lesbian (If I give her the wool will she make me one too?)

Why are the girls kept in when it's the boys who cause all the trouble?

Marriage is a gamble – heads he wins, tails you lose

A woman's place is in the home (I wish I had a home to go to)

A house doesn't need a wife any more than it needs a husband

What's so special about Christmas – the birth of a man who thinks he's a god isn't such a rare event

I became a feminist as an alternative to becoming a masochist

If ignorance is bliss then men have reached Nirvana

Stamp out rape – keep men off the streets

An Englishman's home is his castle – so let him clean it

Eve was the first feminist – she tried to bring about the fall of man

Why are girls called birds? Because they pick up worms

Does the iron lady use Brillo pads? Only her gynometallurgist knows for sure

No darling – it only leads to housework

Little girl, little girl where have you been?

I've been up to London to model for *Queen*.
Little girl, little girl, what did you there?
Stood around, leapt around, jumped around, bare.
Little girl, little girl, what happened then?
Nothing – they're funny these cameramen.

When God made man she was having one of her off-days

Women say 'no' to male violence – Men say 'No' to female graffiti

Manslaughter is a terrible thing – Womanslaughter is even worse

Women who seek equality with men lack ambition

When God made man she was only joking – and woman was the punchline

Cupid's aim is straight but he still makes a lot of Mrs

If this car was a woman she would get her bottom pinched.
If this woman was a car she'd run you down

Women in labour keep capital in power

What do I have to give you to get a kiss? Chloroform

Castrate rapists . . . have a ball!

Equality is a myth – No, it's a Ms

Disarm all rapists – it's not their arms I'm worried about

Only the woman whose neck is bent will bear the oppressor's heel

For feminine protection – use a hand grenade

Women – get out from under

Joan of Arc proved that the sword is mightier than the pen

Telepathising woman seeks another for radio-jamming the patriarchy

Are you a practising lesbian? No, this is about as good as I get.

Everyone's pink on the inside

How about herstory for a change!

Were women born only to procreate and rot?

Woman was born free, but everywhere she is in chains.
Man was born free but women are more expensive.

Women's bodies belong to themselves – but isn't it nice to share?

Before you meet your handsome prince – you have to kiss an awful lot of toads

There is only one thing that men do better than women – rape

What would the world be without men? Free of crime and full of fat, happy women.

He's very sweet . . . but I'm on a diet

Renew his interest in carpentry . . . saw his head off

Say it with flowers . . . give him a triffid

Which of us is the opposite sex?

Women have many faults – men have only two – everything they say and everything they do

Women like the simpler things in life – like men

The tròuble with the world is that so many political jokes get elected

I was born a woman . . . I won't be told how to become one

Don't put me on a pedestal and then expect me to dust it

Make love not war – I'm married – I do both

It begins when you sink in his arms . . . it ends with your arms in his sink

My husband made me happy by adding some magic to our marriage – he disappeared

I used to find him boring until I stopped listening

The dinner's in the cat

A woman's lot is not a nappy one

An employed housewife gets two jobs for the price of one

What have you got in common with your husband? We were both married on the same day.

When you've Adam don't they make you eve?

When women start to act like human beings they are accused of trying to be men

Being a mother is always having to say you're sorry

Adam came first – but men always do

The waltz was invented by men – for them to lead and step on the woman at the same time

Make love during the safe period – when her husband's away

What's the difference between nice women and garbage? Garbage gets taken out at least once a week.

AGE

RUTH ADAM

When I was young I was frightened I might bore people, now I'm old I am frightened they will bore me.

LISA ALTHER (*b.* 1944)
American writer
In *Kinflicks*

If this was adulthood, the only improvement she could detect in her situation was that now she could eat dessert without eating her vegetables.

ELIZABETH ARDEN (*c.* 1884–1966)
Canadian beautician

I'm not interested in age. People who tell their age are silly. You're as old as you feel.

LADY CYNTHIA ASQUITH (1887–1960)
British writer

Oh, why was I born for this time? Before one is thirty to know more dead than living people.

LADY ASTOR (NANCY) (1879–1964)
First woman MP

I refuse to admit I'm more than fifty-two even if that does make my sons illegitimate.

LAUREN BACALL (*b.* 1924)
American actress

The good still die young. Eternal youth – that's what you need. Nothing improves with age.

BRIGITTE BARDOT (*b.* 1933)
French actress

It's sad to grow old, but nice to ripen.

What could be more beautiful than a dear old lady growing wise with age? Every age can be enchanting, provided you live within it.

I have noticed signs of ageing in the last two years and even feel a little frightened when a new wrinkle appears.

ETHEL BARRYMORE (1879–1959)
American actress

You grow up the day you have the first real laugh – at yourself.

NINA BAWDEN (*b.* 1925)
English novelist
In *A Woman of My Age*

Before we came away, I bought a special cream supposed to restore elasticity to the skin, but I destroyed the wrapper on the jar and the accompanying, incriminating literature, as furtively as I had, when young, removed the cover of a book on sex.

SIMONE DE BEAUVOIR (*b.* 1908)
French writer

Never, on any plane, does the aged person lapse into a 'second childhood', since childhood is, by definition, a forward, upward movement.

Age changes our relationship with time: as the years go by our future shortens, while our pasts grow heavier.

JEAN-PAUL BELMONDO (*b.* 1933)
French film star

Women over thirty are at their best, but men over thirty are too old to recognise it.

CANDICE BERGEN (*b.* 1946)
American actress

I can't think of anything grimmer than being an ageing actress – God! it's worse than being an ageing homosexual.

LADY BESSBOROUGH (1761–1821)

There is no surer sign of humility than boasting of compliments. A vain person thinks them their due.

CATHERINE BRAMWELL BOOTH (*b.* 1883)
Salvation Army Commissioner
On the eve of her 100th birthday

It's a strange experience to live so near to death. You find yourself planning something, then you pull yourself up and think, 'I may not be here' . . . I'm in love with living.

CATHERINE DRINKER BOWEN (1897–1973)
American biologist and essayist

I speak the truth, not so much as I would, but as much as I dare; and I dare a little more, as I grow older.

PEARL S. BUCK (1892–1973)
American novelist

Perhaps one has to be very old before one learns to be amused rather than shocked.

ROBERT BURNS (1759–1796)
Scottish poet

What can a young lassie, what shall a young lassie,
What can a young lassie do wi' an auld man?

LORD BYRON (1788–1824)
British poet
In *Don Juan*

A lady of a 'certain age', which means
Certainly aged.

On Marguerite, Countess Blessington

She is also very pretty even in the morning . . . Miladi seems highly literary. Certainly English women wear better than their continental neighbours of the same sex.

BILLY CARTER
Brother of former US President Jimmy Carter

There's nothing in the world you can do with a seventy-five-year-old woman but be nice to her.

MRS LILLIAN CARTER (*d.* 1983)
Mother of former US President Jimmy Carter
(While in her seventies)

Sure I'm for helping the elderly. I'm going to be old myself someday.

COCO CHANEL (Gabrielle) (1883–1971)
French couturière
On reaching sixty

Cut off my head and I am thirteen.

Youth is something very new. Twenty years ago no one mentioned it.

Nature gives you the face you have at twenty, but it's up to you to merit the face you have at fifty.

CHER (*b.* 1946)
American singer

Getting married and getting old are the two things that save everybody's ass.

AGATHA CHRISTIE (1891–1976)
British thriller writer, married to archaeologist Sir Max Mallowan

An archaeologist is the best husband any woman can have; the older she gets, the more interested he is in her.

SARAH CHURCHILL (1914–1982)
Actress daughter of Sir Winston Churchill

As long as you can still be disappointed, you are still young.

LADY DIANA COOPER (*b.* 1892)
British aristocrat

Age wins and one must learn to grow old.

Age is an ugly thing, and it goes on getting worse.

DORIS DAY (*b.* 1924)
American actress

The really frightening thing about middle age is the knowledge that you'll grow out of it.

SHELAGH DELANEY (*b.* 1939)
Irish playwright
In *A Taste of Honey*

Women never have young minds. They are born 3000 years old.

MARLENE DIETRICH (*b.* 1901)
German-born actress

Say I am seventy-five and let it go at that.

CHRISTIAN DIOR (1905–1957)
French couturièr

Women are most fascinating between the ages of thirty-five and forty, after they have won a few races and know how to pace themselves. Since few women ever pass forty, maximum fascination can continue indefinitely.

MADAME DE DINO

After the age of eighty, all contemporaries are friends.

FERN MARIA ECKMAN
On Queen Elizabeth II

She is a woman who acts her age, which is fifty. She has, in fact, acted that age since she was little more than twenty.

DAME EDITH EVANS (1888–1976)
British actress

I may never have been very pretty but I was jolly larky and that's what counts in the theatre.

ROBERT FROST (1874–1963)
American poet

A diplomat is a man who always remembers a woman's birthday but never remembers her age.

JUDY GARLAND (1922–1969)
American actress

I was born at the age of twelve on a Metro-Goldwyn-Mayer lot.

RUTH GORDON (*b.* 1896)
American actress

When you finally learn how to do it, you're too old for the good parts.

JANE ELLEN HARRISON (1850–1938)

Life does not cease when you are old, it only suffers a rich change. You go on loving, only your love, instead of a burning, fiery furnace, is the mellow glow of an autumn sun.

LILLIAN HELLMAN (1907–1984)
American playwright

Nothing, of course, begins at the time you think it did.

KATHARINE HEPBURN (*b.* 1909)
American actress

If you survive long enough, you're revered – rather like an old building.

The male sex, as a sex, does not universally appeal to me. I find the men today less manly; but a woman of my age is not in a position to know exactly how manly they are.

SANDRA HOCHMAN

I gave my life to learning how to live. Now that I have organised it all . . . It is just about over.

EDGAR WATSON HOWE (1853–1937)

A woman is as old as she looks before breakfast.

DR SAMUEL JOHNSON (1709–1784)
British writer

So, when female minds are embittered by age or solitude, their malignity is generally exerted in a rigorous and spiteful superintendence of domestic trifles.

HELEN KELLER (1880–1968)
Writer and lecturer (born deaf and blind)

Fact and fancy look alike across the years that link the past with the present.

ELSA LANCHESTER (*b.* 1902)
British-born actress

It's a damned nuisance getting older, but it's not exactly depressing.

GYPSY ROSE LEE (1914–1970)
American stripper

I have everything now I had twenty years ago – except now it's all lower.

NINON DE LENCLOS (1620–1705)
French society hostess and patron

Old age is woman's hell.

DORIS LESSING (*b.* 1919)
British writer

All one's life as a young woman one is on show, a focus of

attention, people notice you. You set yourself up to be noticed and admired. And then, not expecting it, you become middle-aged and anonymous. No one notices you. You achieve a wonderful freedom. It is a positive thing. You can move about, unnoticed and invisible.

LOELIA, DUCHESS OF WESTMINSTER (*b.* 1902)

Anyone seen on a bus after the age of thirty has been a failure in life.

ELISABETH LUTYENS (1906–1983)
British composer

You're avant-garde for twenty years, then suddenly you're an old-fashioned floozie.

MOMS MABLEY
American actress
On old age

You just wake up one morning, and you got it!

ANNA MAGNANI (*b.* 1909)
Italian actress
To a photographer

Please don't retouch my wrinkles. It took me so long to earn them.

COLLEEN MCCULLOUGH
Australian writer

The lovely thing about being forty is that you can appreciate twenty-five-year-old men more.

MIGNON MCLAUGHLIN
American writer

The young can seldom be faithless for long to the same person.

How it rejoices a middle-aged woman when her husband criticizes a pretty girl.

MARGARET MEAD (1901–1978)
American anthropologist

Young people are moving away from feeling guilty about sleeping with somebody to feeling guilty if they are *not* sleeping with someone.

GOLDA MEIR (1898–1978)
Israeli politician

Old age is like a plane flying through a storm. Once you're aboard there's nothing you can do.

Being seventy is not a sin.

DOROTHY REED MENDENHALL (1874–1964)
American physician

The worst thing about old age is the rapidity with which your periphery sinks.

GEORGE JEAN NATHAN (1882–1958)
American critic

Women, as they grow older, rely more and more on cosmetics. Men, as they grow older, rely more and more on a sense of humour.

MARY PICKFORD (1893–1979)
American actress

People remember me most as a little girl with long golden curls. I don't want them to see me as a little old lady.

MARY QUANT (*b.* 1934)
British fashion designer

A woman is as young as her knees.

GAIL SHEEHY (*b.* 1937)
American journalist

When men reach their sixties and retire they go to pieces. Women just go right on cooking.

RICHARD BRINSLEY SHERIDAN (1751–1816)
Irish-born playwright
In *The School for Scandal*

Here's to the maiden of bashful fifteen;
  Here's to the widow of fifty;
Here's to the flaunting, extravagant quean;
  And here's to the housewife that's thrifty.
    Let the toast pass, –
    Drink to the lass,
I'll warrant she'll prove an excuse for a glass.

MRS PEARSALL SMITH
In a letter from Logan Pearsall Smith's *A Religious Rebel*

We are in 1903 and I am nearly seventy-one years old. I always thought I should love to grow old, and I find it is even more delightful than I thought. It is so delicious to be done with things, and to feel no need any longer to concern myself much about earthly affairs. I seem on the verge of a most delightful journey to a place of unknown joys and pleasures, and things here seem of so little importance compared to things there, that they have lost most of their interest for me . . .

JAMES STEPHENS (1882–1950)
British writer

Men come of age at sixty, women at fifteen.

GRACE SLICK (*b.* 1939)
American rock singer

Are women my age supposed to sing rock 'n' roll?

JONATHAN SWIFT (1667–1745)
English writer

I swear, she's no chicken; she's on the wrong side of thirty, if she be a day.

ELIZABETH TAYLOR (1912–1975)
British writer
In *A Wreath of Roses*

It is very strange . . . that the years teach us patience; that the shorter our time, the greater our capacity for waiting.

ELIZABETH TAYLOR (*b.* 1932)
British-born actress

It seems the older men get, the younger their new wives get.

H. W. THOMPSON (*b.* 1908)
British academic

An old man marrying a young girl is like buying a book for someone else to read.

JEAN-BAPTISTE TROISGROS
In *New York Times*, 24 October 1974

From thirty-five to forty-five women are old, and at forty-five the devil takes over, and they're beautiful, splendid, maternal, proud. The acidities are gone, and in their place reigns calm. They are worth going out to find, and because of them some men never grow old. When I see them my mouth waters.

SOPHIE TUCKER (1884–1966)
American singer
Song Title

Life begins at forty.

FAY WELDON (*b.* 1932)
British writer

Man seems not so much wicked as frail, unable to face pain, trouble and growing old. A good woman knows that nature is her enemy. Look at what it does to her.

MAE WEST (1882–1980)
American film star

Women are as old as they feel – and men are old when they lose their feelings.

You're never too old to become younger.

OSCAR WILDE (1854–1900)
Irish writer
In *A Woman of No Importance*

One should never trust a woman who tells one her real age. A woman who would tell one that would tell one anything.

In *The Importance of Being Earnest*

No woman should ever be quite accurate about her age. It looks so calculating.

Thirty-five is a very attractive age. London Society is full of women of the very highest birth who have, of their own free choice, remained thirty-five for years.

DEATH

AGRIPPINA
Mother of Emperor Nero (AD 37–68) who committed suicide

Smite my womb!

ZOË AKINS (*b.* 1886)
In *The Portrait of Tiero*

Nothing seems so tragic to one who is old as the death of one who is young, and this alone proves that life is a good thing.

LOUISA MAY ALCOTT (1832–1888)
American writer
Last words

Is it not meningitis?

QUEEN ANNE (1665–1714)
On handing the staff of the Treasury to Lord Shrewsbury.

Use it for the good of my people.

LADY ASTOR (NANCY) (1879–1964)
On seeing all her children assembled in her last illness

Am I dying, or is this my birthday?

Her epitaph at Kensal Green

Here England buries her grudge against Columbus.

JANE AUSTEN (1775–1817)
On being asked what she required

Nothing but death.

MARTHA BECK (*d.* 1951)
American murderer, who was executed

My story is a love story, but only those who are tortured by love can understand what I mean. I was pictured as a fat, unfeeling woman. True, I am fat, but if that is a crime, how many of my sex are guilty? I am not unfeeling, stupid or moronic. My last words and my last thoughts are: Let him who is without sin cast the first stone.

MARY BELL
Eleven-year-old murderer
1963

Murder isn't that bad. We all die sometime.

ROBERT BENCHLEY
On the death of a promiscuous actress

She sleeps alone at last.

CONSTANCE BENNETT (*d.* 1965)
Suggesting her own epitaph

Do not disturb.

SAINT BERNADETTE OF LOURDES (1844–1879)
Last words

Blessed Mary Mother of God pray for me a poor sinner. A poor sinner.

MARY BLANDY
Hanged for poisoning her father, 1752

Gentlemen, don't hang me high for the sake of decency – I am afraid I shall fall.

ANNE BOLEYN (*c.* 1507–1536)
Beheaded

The executioner is, I believe, an expert . . . and my neck is very slender. Oh God, have pity on my soul!

ELIZABETH BOWEN (1899–1973)
Anglo-Irish writer
In *The Death of the Heart*

The heart may think it knows better: the senses know that absence blots people out. We have really no absent friends.

ANNE BRONTË (1820–1849)
British novelist
Last words, to her sister

Take courage, Charlotte, take courage!

CHARLOTTE BRONTË (1816–1855)
Last words. She had been married for one year

Oh, I am not going to die, am I? He will not separate us, we have been so happy.

EMILY BRONTË (1818–1848)
British novelist and poet
In *Remembrance*

Cold in the earth – and the deep snow piled above thee,
Far, far removed, cold in the dreary grave!
Have I forgot, my only Love, to love thee,
Severed at last by Time's all-severing wave?

Now, when alone, do my thoughts no longer hover
Over the mountains, on that northern shore,
Resting their wings where heath and fern-leaves cover
Thy noble heart for ever, ever more?

On her deathbed

If you will send for the doctor, I will see him now.

ELIZABETH BARRETT BROWNING (1806–1861)
On being asked how she was feeling

Beautiful.

FRANCES HODGSON BURNETT (1843–1924)
British novelist
Last words

With the best that was in me I have tried to write more happiness into the world.

JANE WELSH CARLYLE (1801–1866)

Never does one feel oneself so utterly helpless as in trying to speak comfort for great bereavement. I will not try it. Time is the only comforter for the loss of a mother.

QUEEN CAROLINE (1683–1737)
Wife of George II
Last words

Pray louder that I may hear.

CATHERINE OF ARAGON (1485–1536)
Wife of Henry VIII
Last words

Lord into Thy hands I commend my spirit.

EDITH CAVELL (1865–1915)
British nurse
Shot by the Germans for helping English and French soldiers to escape during World War I

I realize that patriotism is not enough. I must have no hatred or bitterness towards anyone.

COCO CHANEL (GABRIELLE) (1883–1971)
Last words quoted in Edmonde Charles-Roux's *Chanel*

So that's how you die.

CHARLOTTE AUGUSTA (1796–1817)
Princess of Wales
Calling for Baron Stockmar, during her death in childbirth

They have made me tipsy. Stocky, Stocky!

CHRISTINA (1626–1689)
Queen of Sweden
Dictating the inscription on her gravestone

Queen Christina lived LXIII years.

COLETTE (Sidonie-Gabrielle) (1873–1954)
French novelist
In *Earthly Paradise* ('The Captain')

It takes time for the absent to assume their true shape in our thoughts. After death they take on a firmer outline and then cease to change.

CHARLOTTE CORDAY (1768–1793)
Assassin of Marat
On gazing at the guillotine

I have a right to be curious, I have never seen one before. It is the toilette of death, but it leads to immortality.

MARIE CURIE (1867–1934)
On being offered an injection to ease her pain

I don't want it.

VARINA H. DAVIS (*d.* 1898)
Wife of Jefferson Davis
Last words

Oh Lord in Thee have I trusted. Let me not be confounded.

EMILY DICKINSON (1830–1886)
American poet

Death is the supple Suitor
That wins at last
It is a stealthy Wooing
Conducted first
By pallid innuendoes
And dim approach
But brave at last with Bugles.

When dying and being offered a glass of water
I must go in, the fog is rising. Oh, is that all it is?

BENJAMIN DISRAELI (1804–1881)
In *Reminiscences*

The Queen (Victoria) talked freely of the Prince; he *would* die. . . . Then she used these words, 'He died from want of what they call pluck.'

JOHN DRYDEN
English poet
Proposing an epitaph for his wife, Lady Elizabeth Dryden (1638–1714)

Here lies my wife
Here let her lie!
Now she's at rest
And so am I.

ISADORA DUNCAN (1878–1927)
American dancer
Killed in a car accident

Adieu my friends, I go on to glory!

ELEANORA DUSE (1859–1924)
Italian actress
Last words

We must stir ourselves. Move on! Work, work! Cover me! Must move on! Must work! Cover me!

JEANNE EAGELS (*d.* 1929)
Actress

I'm going to Dr Caldwell's for one of my regular treatments.

AMELIA EARHART (1898–1937)
American airwoman
In her last letter to her husband.
She disappeared while making a Pacific flight

Please know that I am quite aware of the hazards. I want to do it because I want to do it. Women must try to do things as men have tried. When they fail, their failure must be but a challenge to others.

MARY BAKER EDDY (1821–1910)
Founder of the Christian Science movement
Last words

God is my life.

GEORGE ELIOT (Marian Evans) (1819–1880)
British writer

Worldly faces never look so worldly as at a funeral.

Last words

Tell them I have a great pain in the left side.

QUEEN ELIZABETH I (1533–1603)
Last words to Robert Cecil who insisted she go to bed

Must! Is must a word to be addressed to princes? Little man, little man! Thy father, if he had been alive, durst not have used that word. All my possessions for one moment of time.

'MADAME' ELIZABETH
Sister of Louis XVI
Guillotined, 1794

In the name of modesty, cover my bosom.

EPITAPH
Hatfield, Massachusetts

Beneath this stone, a lump of clay
Lies Arabella Young
Who on the 21st of May
Began to hold her tongue.

EPITAPH
Kilmurry, Ireland

This stone was raised by Sarah's lord,
Not Sarah's virtues to record –
For they're well known to all the town –
But it was raised to keep her down.

DAME EDITH EVANS (1888–1976)
British actress
In a BBC Radio interview, a week before her death on 14 October

Death is my neighbour now.

KATHLEEN FERRIER (1912–1953)
British singer

Now I'll have *eine kleine* pause.

RONALD FIRBANK (1886–1926)
English novelist
In *The Eccentricities of Cardinal Pirelli*

She made a ravishing corpse.

ELIZABETH FRY (1780–1845)
British philanthropist
Last words

Oh dear Lord, help and keep Thy servant.

MRS DAVID GARRICK (*d.* 1822)
When offered a cup of tea by a maid

Put it down, hussy! Do you think I cannot help myself?

FANNY GODWIN
Illegitimate daughter of Mary Wollstonecraft and Captain Imlay
Suicide note

I have long determined that the best thing I could do was to put an end to the existence of a being whose birth was unfortunate, and whose life has only been a series of pains to those persons who have hurt their health in endeavouring to promote her welfare. Perhaps to hear of my death may give you pain, but you will soon have the blessing of forgetting that such a creature ever existed.

RUTH GORDON (*b.* 1896)
American actress

In our family we don't divorce our men – we bury them.

LADY JANE GREY (1537–1554)
Beheaded for attempting to usurp the throne

I die in peace with all people. God save the Queen.

TEXAS (MARY L.) GUINAN
American nightclub hostess

I want to lie in state at Campbell's. I want for once to give the people a chance to see me without a cover charge.

HELOISE (*d.* 1164)
Lover of Abelard

In death at last let me rest with Abelard.

(Now buried together at Père Lachaise cemetery, Paris)

EPITAPH
Hollis, New Hampshire, USA

Here lies Cynthia, Steven's wife,
She lived six years in calm and strife.
Death came at last and set her free,
I was glad and so was she.

WINIFRED HOLTBY (1839–1935)
British novelist
Inscription on her grave

God give me work while I may live and life till my work is done.

CATHERINE HOWARD (*d.* 1542)
Wife of Henry VIII
Executed for adultery with Thomas Culpepper

I die a Queen, but I would rather die the wife of Culpepper. God have mercy on my soul. Good people, I beg you pray for me.

JULIA WARD HOWE (*d.* 1910)
Composer of *The Battle Hymn of the Republic*
Last words

God will help me . . . I am so tired!

ANNE HYDE (*d.* 1671)
Duchess of York, mother of Queen Mary and Queen Anne
Last words

Truth! Truth!

ISABELLA (1451–1504)
Queen of Castille

Do not weep for me, nor waste your time in fruitless prayers for my recovery, but pray rather for the salvation of my soul.

JOAN OF ARC (1412–1431)
Burned at the stake

Ah Rouen, I have great fear that you are going to suffer by my death. Jesus, Jesus!

JANIS JOPLIN (1943–1970)
American rock singer
On the death of Jimi Hendrix 1970

Godammit! He beat me to it.

People like their blues singers dead.

JOSEPHINE (1763–1814)
Empress of France, divorced by Napoleon who then married Marie Louise of Austria

Napoleon! Elba! Marie Louise!

PRINCESS DE LAMBRALLE (*d.* 1792)
Asked by French revolutionary mob to cry '*Vive la nation!*'

Fie on the horror.

She was then torn to pieces by the crowd

GERTRUDE LAWRENCE (1898–1952)
British stage star who died during the Broadway run of *The King and I*

See that Yul [Brynner] gets star billing. He has earned it.

MARY WILSON LITTLE

In some parts of Ireland the sleep which knows no waking is always followed by a wake which knows no sleeping.

MADAME LOUISE (*d.* 1800)
Daughter of Louis XV
Last words

Hurry! At a gallop! To Paradise!

LOUISA (1776–1810)
Queen of Prussia
Last words

I am a Queen, but I have no power to move my arms.

MARY LYON (*d.* 1849)
American educator

I should love to come back to watch over the seminary, but God will take care of it.

KATHERINE MANSFIELD (1890–1923)
New Zealand-born writer
Last words

I believe . . . I'm going to die. I love the rain. I want the feeling of it on my face.

MARIA THERESA (1717–1780)
Austrian empress

I could sleep, but must not give way to it. Death is so near, he must not be allowed to steal upon me unawares. For fifteen years I have been making ready for him, and must meet him awake.

MARIA THERESA OF FRANCE (*d.* 1682)
On the fact that it was raining outside

Yes, it is indeed frightful weather for a journey as long as the one before me.

MARIE ANTOINETTE (1755–1793)
Queen of France
Having tripped over her executioner's foot

Monsieur, I beg your pardon. I did not do it on purpose.

HARRIET MARTINEAU (1802–1876)
English writer and reformer

I have had a noble share of life and I do not ask for any other life. I see no reason why the existence of Harriet Martineau should be perpetuated.

MARY QUEEN OF SCOTS (1542–1587)
Executed
To her waiting women

Do not cry. I have prayed for you. In You, Lord, I have faith, and You shall protect me for ever. Into Thy hands, O Lord, I commend my spirit.

MARY I (1516–1558)
Queen of England

When I am dead and opened, you shall find 'Calais' lying in my heart.

CATHERINE DE MEDICI (1519–1589)
Wife of Henry II of France

Ah, my God, I am dead!

ALICE MEYNELL (*d.* 1922)
English poet

This is not tragic. I am happy.

EDNA ST VINCENT MILLAY (1892–1950)
American poet
In *Keen*

Blessed be Death, that cuts in marble
What would have sunk to dust!

Heap not on this mound
Roses that she loved so well;
Why bewilder her with roses,
That she cannot see or smell?

The rain has such a friendly sound
To one who's six feet underground.

ARTHUR MILLER
American playwright. Former husband of Marilyn Monroe
(Attr.) On Marilyn Monroe's funeral, August 1962

Why should I go? She won't be there.

JESSICA MITFORD
On her sister, Nancy Mitford's death

I have nothing against undertakers personally. It's just that I wouldn't want one to bury my sister.

MARIA MONTESSORI (1870–1952)
Italian educationalist
Last words

Am I no longer any use, then?

HORATIA NELSON (1801–1881)
Daughter of Lord Nelson and Lady Hamilton
On her mother's last illness

Lady Hamilton took little interest in anything but the indulgence of her unfortunate habit, and after the first week of her removal to the lodgings she hired in Calais at Monsieur Damas, but once she left her bed. . . . at that time I never went out no one could have called unknown to me and I hardly ever during the day left her room, my own almost opened into it. For some time before she died she was not kind to me, but she had much to try her alas to spite her, and I was too well aware of the state of her finances, so much so that I applied to Lord Nelson to advance me a portion of my dividend for use in providing necessaries for the house.

MARGARET, DUCHESS OF NEWCASTLE (1624–1673)
Epitaph, Westminster Abbey

Her name was Margaret Lucas, youngest sister to the Lord Lucas of Colchester, a noble familie; for all the Brothers were Valiant, and all the Sisters virtuous.

FLORENCE NIGHTINGALE (1820–1910)
On being handed the Order of Merit on her deathbed

Too kind – too kind.

DOROTHY PARKER (1893–1967)
American writer and wit
In *Enough Rope*

Death will not see me flinch;
the heart is bold
That pain has made incapable of pain.

To Beatrice Ames, a few days before her lonely death

I want you to tell me the truth. Did Ernest (Hemingway) really like me?

DOROTHY W. PATTISON (*d.* 1878)
Philanthropist

I have lived alone, let me die alone, let me die alone.

ANNA PAVLOVA (1885–1931)
Russian ballet dancer
Last words

Get my Swan costume ready.

SYLVIA PLATH (1932–1963)
American poet, who committed suicide

Dying
Is an art, like everything else.
I do it exceptionally well.

MADAME DE POMPADOUR (1721–1764)
Mistress of Louis XV
As the priest was leaving her room

One moment, Monsieur le Curé, and we will depart together.

ROSE RODIN (*d.* 1917)
Wife of the sculptor

I don't mind dying, but it's leaving my man. Who will look after him. What will happen to the poor thing?

ELEANOR ROOSEVELT (1884–1962)
Wife of the 32nd President of the United States
In a letter, 1960

When you cease to make a contribution you begin to die.

ETHEL ROSENBERG
Electrocuted in the United States for alleged spying, 1943

We are the first victims of American fascism.

ELISABETH KÜBLER-ROSS

Death is simply a shedding of the physical body, like the butterfly coming out of a cocoon. It is a transition into a higher state of consciousness, where you continue to perceive, to understand, to laugh, to be able to grow, and the only thing you lose is something that you don't need anymore . . . your physical body. It's like putting away your winter coat when spring comes.

CHRISTINA ROSSETTI (1830–1894)
English poet

I love everybody. If ever I had an enemy I should hope to meet and welcome that enemy in heaven.

When I am dead, my dearest,
Sing no sad songs for me.

Better by far you should forget and smile
Than that you should remember and be sad.

SAPPHO (*d.* 7th century BC)
A farewell poem to her daughter

For it is not right that in the house of song there be mourning. Such things befit not us.

CLARA SCHUMANN (1819–1896)
German concert pianist, wife of Robert Schumann

I always wish that the last movement [of the Regenlieder Sonata] might accompany me in my journey from here to the next world.

MARY-ANNE SCHIMMELPENNINCK (*d.* 1856)
Writer of children's books

Oh, I hear such beautiful voices, and the children are the loudest.

JEAN SEBERG
American film star
Suicide note, 1979

I can't live any longer with my nerves.

ARABELLA EUGENIA SMITH (1845–1916)
In *If I Should Die Tonight*

If I should die tonight,
My friends would look upon my quiet face,
Before they laid it in its resting place.
And deem that death had left it almost fair.

JOANNA SOUTHCOTT (*c.* 1750–1814)
English religious fanatic

If I have been deceived, doubtless it was the work of a spirit. Whether the spirit was good or bad I do not know.

MADAME DE STAËL (1766–1817)
French author
On being asked if she would sleep
Heavily, like a big peasant woman.

GERTRUDE STEIN (1874–1946)
American author

Just before she died, she asked, 'What is the answer?' No answer came. She laughed and said, 'In that case, what is the question?'

LUCY STONE (*d.* 1893)
Suffragette
Last words

Make the world better!

MRS ISADORE STRAUS
On the *Titanic*, 1912.
Refusing to take a lifeboat which would have parted her from her husband

We have been together for forty years, and we will not separate now.

SAINT TERESA (1515–1582)

Over my spirit flash and float in divine radiancy the bright and glorious visions of the world to which I go.

DAME ELLEN TERRY (1847–1928)
British actress
Scribbled in the dust of her bedside table.

Happy.

ALICE B. TOKLAS
On Gertrude Stein's death in Margo Jefferson's *Passionate Friends*

I wish to God we had gone together as I always so fatuously thought we would – a bomb – shipwreck – just anything but this.

LILY TOMLIN (*b.* 1939)
American comedienne

There will be sex after death – we just won't be able to feel it.

MADAME TUSSAUD (1760–1850)
French wax modeller
To her two sons

I divide my property equally between you, and implore you, above all things, never to quarrel.

QUEEN VICTORIA (1819–1901)
In her *Diary*, 11 June 1870
On the death of Charles Dickens

He is a very great loss. He had a large loving mind and the strongest sympathy with the poorer classes. He felt sure a better feeling, and much greater union of classes, would take place in time. And I pray earnestly it may.

Last words.

Oh that peace may come. Bertie!

SYLVIA TOWNSEND WARNER (*b.* 1893)
English writer
Epitaph

John Bird, a labourer, lies here,
Who served the earth for sixty year
With spade and mattock, drill and plough;
But never found it kind till now.

MARY, COUNTESS OF WARWICK (*d.* 1679)
To her attendants

Well ladies, if I were but one hour in heaven, I would not again be with you, much as I love you.

ETHEL WATERS (*d.* 1977)

I'm not afraid to die, honey. In fact I'm kind of looking forward to it. I know that the Lord has his arms wrapped around this big, fat sparrow.

SARAH WESLEY (1726–1822)
Wife of Charles Wesley, English hymn writer

Open the gates! Open the gates!

KATHERINE WHITEHORN
British journalist

In heaven they will bore you, in hell you will bore them.

VIRGINIA WOOLF (1882–1941)
British writer
Who committed suicide by drowning
In a note for her husband, Leonard Woolf

I have a feeling I shall go mad. I cannot go on any longer in these terrible times. I hear voices and cannot concentrate on my work. I have fought against it but cannot fight any longer. I owe all my happiness to you, but cannot go on and spoil your life.

MEN ON WOMEN

HENRY BROOKS ADAMS (1838–1918)
American historian

Women have, commonly, a very positive moral sense; that which they will is right; that which they reject is wrong; and their will, in most cases, ends by settling the moral.

The woman who is known only through a man is known wrong.

RICHARD ALDINGTON (1892–1962)
British novelist and poet

Forgetting is woman's first and greatest art.

THOMAS BAILEY ALDRICH (1836–1906)
American writer and poet

The ability to have our own way, and at the same time convince others they are having their own way, is a rare thing among man. Among women it is as common as eyebrows.

MUHAMMAD ALI (*b.* 1942)
American boxer

The woman is the fibre of the nation. She is the producer of life. A nation is only as good as its women.

I don't know of any young man, black or white, who doesn't have a girlfriend besides his wife. Some have four sneaking around.

WOODY ALLEN (*b.* 1935)
American actor and writer

She was the type that would wake up in the morning and *immediately* start apologizing.

FRED ALLEN (1894–1956)
American actor

A gentleman is any man who wouldn't hit a woman with his hat on.

KINGSLEY AMIS (*b.* 1932)
British writer

Women are really much nicer than men.
No wonder we like them.

ARISTOPHANES (446–380 BC)
Greek playwright
In *Lysistrata*

These impossible women! How they do get around us!
The poet was right: can't live with them, or without them.

MICHAEL ARLEN (1895–1956)
British novelist
In *Portrait of a Lady on Park Avenue*

Well, emotionally she was unimportant, like a play by Mr Noël Coward, but her construction was faultless, like a play by Mr Noël Coward.

BARBEY D'AUREVILLY (early 19th century)
French man of letters

Next to the wound, what women make best is the bandage.

WALTER BAGEHOT (1826–1877)
British economist and journalist

Men who do not make advances to women are apt to become victims to women who make advances to them.

HONORÉ DE BALZAC (1799–1850)
French novelist

Men are so made that they can resist sound argument, and yet yield to a glance.

J. M. BARRIE (1860–1937)
British playwright
In *What Every Woman Knows*

Every man who is high up likes to feel that he has done it all himself; and the wife smiles, and lets it go at that. It's our only joke. Every woman knows that.

MAX BEERBOHM (1872–1956)
British writer and caricaturist
In *Zuleika Dobson*

She had the air of a born unpacker – swift and firm, yet withal tender. . . . She was one of those born to make chaos cosmic.

She had the sensitiveness, though no other quality whatsoever, of the true artist.

SAUL BELLOW (*b.* 1915)
American writer

All a writer has to do to get a woman is to say he's a writer. It's an aphrodisiac.

ROBERT BENCHLEY (1889–1945)
American writer and critic

Even nowadays a man can't step up and kill a woman without feeling just a bit unchivalrous.

ARNOLD BENNETT (1867–1931)
British novelist

Make love to every woman you meet; if you get five per cent on your outlays it's a good investment.

UGO BETTI (1892–1954)
Italian playwright

When a man makes her laugh, a woman feels protected.

BIBLE

As a jewel of gold in a swine's snout, so is a fair woman which is without direction.

AMBROSE BIERCE (1824–1914)
American journalist
In *The Devil's Dictionary*

When Eve saw her reflection in a pool, she sought Adam and accused him of infidelity.

Women would be the most enchanting creatures on earth if, in falling into their arms one didn't fall into their hands.

MALCOLM BRADBURY (*b.* 1932)
British writer
In *Eating People is Wrong*

It amuses me, you know, the way you seem to see women. You think of them as sort of loose-fitting men.

JUDGE THOMAS P. BRADY

The loveliest and purest of God's creatures, the nearest thing to an angelic being that treads this terrestrial ball, is a well-bred, cultured, Southern white woman, or her blue-eyed, golden-haired little girl.

ERNEST BRAMAH (Smith) (1868–1942)
English novelist
In *Kai Lung Unrolls his Mat*

It is proverbial that from a hungry tiger and an affectionate woman there is no escape.

ROBERT BRIDGES (1844–1930)
British poet

All women born are so perverse
No man need boast their love possessing.

A. CLUTTON BROCK
Member of Parliament

I would warn the wives of eminent men to treat their husbands as if they were not eminent.

RUPERT BROOKE (1887–1915)
British poet

But there's wisdom in women, of more than they have known.
And thoughts go blowing through them, are wiser than their own.

SIR THOMAS BROWN (1605–1682)
In *Religio Medici, I*

The whole world was made for man; but the twelfth part of man for woman; man is the whole world, and the breath of God; woman the rib and crooked piece of man. I could be content that we might procreate like trees, without conjunction, or that there were any way to perpetuate the world without this trivial and vulgar way of union.

JEAN DE LA BRUYÈRE (1645–1696)
French writer

A man keeps another's secret better than he does his own. A woman, on the other hand, keeps her own better than another's.

A man can deceive a woman by his sham attachment to her provided he does not have a real attachment elsewhere.

YUL BRYNNER (*b.* 1915)
American actor

Girls have an unfair advantage over men: if they can't get what they want by being smart, they can get it by being dumb.

HENRY LYTTON BULWER (1801–1872)

There is something very delightful in turning from the unquietness and agitation, the fever, the ambition, the harsh and worldly realities of man's character, to the gentle and deep recesses of woman's more secret heart. Within her musings is a realm of haunted and fairy thought, to which the things of this turbid and troubled life have no entrance. What to her are the changes of state, the rivalries and contentions which form the staple of man's existence? For her there is an intense and fond philosophy, before whose eye substances flit and fade like shadows, and shadows grow glowingly into truth. Her soul's creations are not as the moving and moral images seen in the common day; they are things, like spirits steeped in the dim moonlight, heard when all else are still, and busy when earth's labourers are at rest! Hers is the real and uncentred *poetry of being*, which pervades and surrounds her as with an air, which peoples her visions, and animates her love – which shrinks from earth into itself, and finds marvel and meditation in all that it beholds.

O woman! in ordinary cases so mere a mortal, how, in the great and rare events of life, dost thou swell into the angel.

GELETT BURGESS (1866–1951)
American writer
In *The Maxims of Methuselah*

Verily, men do foolish things thoughtlessly, knowing not why; but no woman doeth aught without a reason.

G. S. BURGIN (1856–1945)
British writer

No woman ever looks exactly what she is: if she did, she'd at once try to be different.

ROBERT BURNS (1759–1796)
Scottish poet

O, gie me the lass that has acres o' charms,
O, gie me the lass wi the weel-stockit farms.

LORD BYRON (1788–1825)
British poet
In his *Journal*, 27 February 1814

There is something to me very softening in the presence of a woman – some strange influence, even if one is not in love with them – which I cannot at all account for, having no very high opinion of the sex. But yet, I always feel in better humour with myself and everything else, if there is a woman within ken.

In *Don Juan*

Now what I love in women is, they won't
Or can't do otherwise than lie, but do it
So well, the very truth seems falsehood to it.

Man's love is of man's life a thing apart,
'Tis woman's whole existence.

I for one venerate a petticoat.

The night
Shows stars and women in a better light.

HALL CAINE (1853–1931)
British novelist
In *The Eternal City*

I reject the monstrous theory that while a man may redeem the past a woman never can.

RAYMOND CHANDLER (1888–1959)
American novelist
In *Farewell, My Lovely*

It was a blonde. A blonde to make a bishop kick a hole in a stained-glass window.

CHARLIE CHAPLIN (1889–1977)
British-born actor and film-maker

Every woman needs a man to discover her.

MALCOLM DE CHAZAL

A woman knows how to keep quiet when she is in the right, whereas a man, when he is in the right, will keep on talking.

G. K. CHESTERTON (1874–1936)
British essayist and novelist

The average woman is at the head of something with which

she can do as she likes; the average man has to obey orders and do nothing else.

Twenty million young women rose to their feet with the cry, 'We will not be dictated to', and promptly became stenographers.

If you convey to a woman that something ought to be done, there is always a dreadful danger that she will suddenly do it.

Women prefer to talk in two's; while men prefer to talk in three's.

A man's friend likes him but leaves him as he is: his wife loves him and is always trying to turn him into somebody else.

MAURICE CHEVALIER (1888–1972)
French singer and actor

Many a man has fallen in love with a girl in a light so dim he would not have chosen a suit by it.

FRANK MOORE COLBY (1865–1925)

Women singly do a good deal of harm. Women in bulk are chastening.

CHARLES CALEB COLTON (1780–1832)
British clergyman and writer

Most females will forgive a liberty rather than a slight.

WILLIAM CONGREVE (1670–1729)
British playwright
In *The Mourning Bride*

Heaven has no rage like love to hatred turned,
Nor hell a fury like a woman scorned.

In *Amoret*

Careless is she with artful care,
Affecting to seem unaffected.

In *The Double-Dealer*

Women, like flames, have a destroying power,
Ne'er to be quenched till they themselves devour.

In *Love For Love*

Women are like tricks by slight of hand,
Which, to admire, we should not understand.

A woman only obliges a man to secrecy, that she may have the pleasure of telling herself.

In *The Old Bachelor*

In my conscience I believe the baggage loves me, for she never speaks well of me herself, nor suffers anybody else to rail at me.

CYRIL CONNOLLY (1903–1974)
British critic

There is no fury like a woman searching for a new lover.

A woman's desire for revenge outlasts all her other emotions.

JOSEPH CONRAD (1857–1925)
Polish-born novelist

The last thing a woman will consent to discover in a man whom she loves, or on whom she simply depends, is want of courage.

WILLIAM COOPER (*b.* 1910)
English novelist
In *Scenes from Provincial Life*

The trouble about finding a husband for one's mistress, is that no other man seems quite good enough.

If girls aren't ignorant, they're cultured . . . You can't avoid suffering.

GEORGES COURTELINE (1860–1929)
French playwright

A woman never sees what we do for her, she only sees what we don't do.

Women are better than they are reputed to be: they don't mock the tears men shed unless they themselves are responsible for them.

NOËL COWARD (1899–1973)
British actor and playwright

American women mostly have their clothes arranged for them. And their faces too, I think.

AUGUST DARNELL
British rock singer (Kid Creole and the Coconuts)

Man will have to advance so many light years before his mind will accept taking orders and direction from a female. But that's what's coming.

Women are awfully volatile. Like faucets they run hot and cold!

MARQUISE DU DEFFAND (1697–1780)
French nobleman and wit

Women are never stronger than when they arm themselves with their weaknesses.

CHARLES DIBDIN (1745–1814)
English dramatist
In *A Love Ditty*

She hath a way so to control
To rapture the imprisoned soul
And sweetest Heaven on earth display,
That to be Heaven Ann hath a way;
She hath a way
Ann Hathaway –
To be Heaven's self Ann hath a way.

CHARLES DICKENS (1812–1870)
British novelist
In *Bleak House*

It's my old girl that advises. She has the head. But I never own to it before her. Discipline must be maintained. (Mr Bagnet)

JOHN DRYDEN (1631–1700)
British poet
In *Alexander's Feast*

None but the brave deserve the fair.

ALEXANDRE DUMAS (1803–1870)
French writer

Cherchez la femme.

LAWRENCE DURRELL (*b.* 1912)
British writer

If you really worship women they'll forgive you everything, even if your balls are dropping off.

JUDGE CLAUDE DUVEEN
'Sayings of the Week' (*Observer*, 9 July 1972)

All Berkshire women are very silly. I don't know why women in Berkshire are more silly than anywhere else.

BOB DYLAN (née Zimmerman) (*b.* 1941)
American singer

It's an honourable thing to change your name – women do it when they're married.

CLOUGH WILLIAMS-ELLIS (1883–1978)
British architect
Quoted in *The Observer*, 1946

Too many homes are built on foundations of crushed women.

RALPH WALDO EMERSON (1803–1882)
American writer

A woman's strength is the unresistible might of weakness.

A woman should always challenge our respect, and never move our compassion.

JOHN ERSKINE (1509–1591)
Scottish reformer

There's a difference between beauty and charm. A beautiful woman is one I notice. A charming woman is one who notices me.

GEORGE FARQUHAR (1678–1707)
British playwright
In *The Constant Couple*

Charming women can true converts make,
We love the precepts for the teacher's sake.

In *The Beaux' Stratagem*

There's some diversion in a talking blockhead; and since a woman must wear chains, I would have the pleasure of hearing 'em rattle a little.

JAMES T. FARRELL (*b.* 1904)
American novelist

Women will go to you because of your intensity.
They will leave you for the same reason.

FEDERICO FELLINI (*b.* 1920)
Italian film director

Freedom, especially a woman's freedom, is a conquest to be made, not a gift to be received. It isn't granted. It must be taken.

JOHN FERRIAR (1761–1815)
English doctor and critic

They know little of human nature who think, that to perform great actions one must necessarily be a great character. So far from that, there may be much more real greatness of mind displayed in the quiet tenor of a woman's life, than in the most brilliant exploits that ever were performed by man.

W. C. FIELDS (1879–1946)
American actor

Women are like elephants to me; I like to look at them, but I wouldn't want to own one.

F. SCOTT FITZGERALD (1896–1940)
American writer

He was one of those men who come in a door and make any woman with them look guilty.

JOHN FLETCHER (1579–1625)
English dramatist
In *Monsieur Thomas*

O woman, perfect woman! what distraction
Was meant to mankind when thou wast made a devil!

THOMAS FORD (*c.* 1580–1648)
English writer

There is a lady sweet and kind,
Was never face so pleased by mind;
I did but see her passing by,
And yet I love her till I die.

JAMES FORDYCE (1720–1796)
Scottish writer and divine
In *Fragments on Women*

Discreet reserve in a woman, like the distances kept by royal personages, contributes to maintain the proper reverence. Most of our pleasures are prized in proportion to the difficulty with which they are obtained.

There is in female youth an attraction, which every man of the least sensibility must perceive, and if assisted by beauty, it becomes irresistible. The power of woman thus far it is in vain to conceal: He that made both sexes manifestly meant it so, from having attempered our hearts to such emotions. Youth and beauty, set off with sweetness and virtue, capacity and discretion – what have they not accomplished?

Women were manifestly intended to be the mothers and formers of a rational and immortal offspring; to be a kind of softer companion, who, by nameless delightful sympathies and endearments might improve our pleasures and soothe our pains; to lighten the load of domestic cares, and by that means leave us more at leisure for rougher labours, or severer studies; and finally, to spread a certain grace and embellishment over human life. To wish to degrade them from so honourable a station, indicates a mixture of ignorance, grossness, and barbarity.

SIGMUND FREUD (1856–1939)
Austrian founder of psychoanalysis

The great question . . . which I have not been able to answer, despite my thirty years in research into the feminine soul, is 'What does a woman want?'

BRUCE JAY FRIEDMAN (*b.* 1930)
American writer
In *Sex and the Lonely Guy*

A Code of Honour – Never approach a friend's girlfriend or wife with mischief as your goal. There are just too many women in the world to justify that sort of dishonourable behaviour. Unless she's *really* attractive.

ERICH FROMM (1900–1980)
German-American psychoanalyst
In *The Art of Loving*

Women are equal because they are not different any more.

CHRISTOPHER FRY (*b.* 1907)
British playwright
In *Curtmantle*

If every man gave up women in God's name.
Where in God's name would be the men
To give up women in a generation's time?

THOMAS FULLER (1608–1661)
English divine
In *Holy and Profane State* ('The Good Wife')

She commandeth her husband, in any equal matter, by constant obeying him.

JOHN KENNETH GALBRAITH (*b.* 1908)
Canadian economist

I feel very angry when I think of brilliant, or even interesting women whose minds are wasted on a home. Better have an affair. It isn't so permanent and you keep your job.

ORTEGA Y GASSET (1883–1955)
Spanish humanist

The best man for a man and the best man for a woman are not the same.

The woman possesses a theatrical exterior and a circumspect interior, while in the man it is the interior which is theatrical. The woman goes to the theatre; the man carries it inside himself and is the impresario of his own life.

JOHN GAY (1685–1732)
English poet
In *The Beggar's Opera*

I must have women. There is nothing unbends the mind like them.

If the heart of a man is depressed with cares,
The mist is dispelled when a woman appears.

Do like other widows – buy yourself weeds, and be cheerful.

In *A New Song of New Similes*

An inconstant woman, tho' she has no chance to be very happy, can never be very unhappy.

JEAN GIRAUDOUX (1882–1944)
French writer

The man who discovers a woman's weakness is like the huntsman in the heat of the day who finds a cool spring. He wallows in it.

Faithful women are all alike. They think only of their fidelity and never of their husbands.
A faithful woman looks to the spring, a good book, perfume, earthquakes, and divine revelation for the experience others find in a lover. They deceive their husbands, so to speak, with the entire world, men excepted.

OLIVER GOLDSMITH (1723–1774)
English poet and dramatist
In *The Vicar of Wakefield*

When lovely woman stoops to folly
  And finds too late that men betray,
What charm can soothe her melancholy?
  What art can wash her guilt away?

I . . . chose my wife, as she did her wedding gown, not for a fine glossy surface, but such qualities as would wear well.

EDMOND and JULES DE GONCOURT (E. 1822–1896, J. 1830–1870)
French diarists

Only the woman of the world is a woman; the rest are females.

RICHARD GORDON (*b.* 1921)
British doctor and author

She was a girl called Wendy, a blonde, but of the arid sort, like the stubble in a wheatfield after a hot harvest.

RÉMY DE GOURMONT (1858–1915)
French poet and novelist

Most men who rail against women are railing at one woman only.

REVEREND BILLY GRAHAM (*b.* 1918)
American preacher

A person guilty of rape should be castrated. That would stop him pretty quick.

ROBERT GRAVES (*b.* 1895)
British poet
In *A Slice of Wedding Cake*

Why have such scores of lovely, gifted girls
  Married impossible men?
Simple self-sacrifice may be ruled out,
  And missionary endeavour, nine times out of ten.

Has God's supply of tolerable husbands
  Fallen, in fact, so low?
Or do I always over-value woman
  At the expense of man?
        Do I?
          It might be so.

JOHANN WOLFGANG VON GOETHE (1749–1832)
German poet

A beautiful and sparkling, but superficial woman rules a wide circle; a woman of real culture a small one.

GREEK PROVERB

A woman prefers a man without money to money without a man.

SACHA GUITRY (1885–1957)
French actor and playwright

When anyone mentions a cultivated woman to me I imagine her with parsley in her ears.

WALTER KNOWLETON GUTMAN
In *Coronet*, March 1960

There is nothing like the ticker-tape except a woman – nothing that promises, hour after hour, day after day, such sudden developments; nothing that disappoints so often or occasionally fulfils with such unbelievable, passionate magnificence.

WILLIAM HAZLITT (1778–1830)
British critic and essayist

A woman's vanity is interested in making the object of her choice the God of her idolatry.

O. HENRY (William Sydney Porter) (1862–1910)
American writer

It takes a man a lifetime to find out about one particular woman, but if he puts in, say, ten years, industrious and curious, he can acquire the general rudiments of the sex.

What a woman wants is what you're out of. She wants more of a thing when it's scarce.

BURTON HILLIS

The only way women could have equal rights nowadays would be to surrender some.

OLIVER WENDELL HOLMES (1809–1894)
American writer

Man has his will – but woman has her way.

When a man holds his tongue it does not signify much. But when a woman dispenses with the office of that mighty member, when she sheathes her natural weapon at a trying moment, it means that she trusts to still more formidable enginery; to tears may be.

THOMAS HOOD (1799–1845)
English poet
In *The Song of the Shirt*

O! men with sisters dear,
O! men with mothers and wives!
It is not linen you're wearing out,
But human creatures' lives!

In *A Reflection*

When Eve upon the first of Men
  The apple press'd with specious cant,
Oh! what a thousand pities then
  That Adam was not Adamant!

JAMES HOWELL (1594–1666)
Welsh writer

One hair of a woman can draw more than a hundred pair of oxen.

ELBERT HUBBARD (1856–1915)
American essayist

A woman will doubt everything you say except it be compliments to herself.

The average woman sees only the weak points in a strong man, and the good points in a weak one.

VICTOR HUGO (1802–1885)
French writer

One of the magnanimities of woman is to yield.

ALDOUS HUXLEY (*b.* 1894)
British writer
In *Point Counter Point*

A good housewife, she knew how to hash up the conversational remains of last night's dinner to furnish out this morning's lunch.

Brought up in an epoch when ladies apparently rolled along on wheels, Mr Quarles was peculiarly susceptible to calves.

HENRIK IBSEN (1828–1906)
Norwegian playwright

In practical life, the woman is judged by man's law, as if she were a man, not a woman.

WASHINGTON IRVING (1783–1859)
American writer

There is in every true woman's heart a spark of heavenly fire, which lies dormant in the broad daylight of prosperity, but which kindles up and beams and blazes in the dark hour of adversity.

Men are always doomed to be duped, not so much by the

arts of the [other] sex as by their own imaginations. They are always wooing goddesses, and marrying mere mortals.

There is something in sickness that breaks down the pride of manhood; that softens the heart, and brings it back to the feelings of infancy. Who that has languished, even in advanced life, in sickness and despondency, who that has pined on a weary bed in the neglect and loneliness of a foreign land; but has thought on the mother 'that looked on his childhood', that smoothed his pillow, and administered to his helplessness. Oh, there is an enduring tenderness in the love of a mother to a son that transcends all other affections of the heart. It is neither to be chilled by selfishness, nor daunted by danger, nor weakened by worthlessness, nor stifled by ingratitude. She will sacrifice every comfort to his convenience; she will surrender every pleasure to his enjoyment; she will glory in his fame, and exult in prosperity: and if adversity overtake him, he will be the dearer to her by misfortune; and if disgrace settle upon his name, she will still love and cherish him; and if all the world beside cast him off, she will be all the world to him.

I have often had occasion to remark the fortitude with which women sustain the most overwhelming reverses of fortune. Those disasters which break down the spirit of a man and prostrate him in the dust, seem to call forth all the energies of the softer sex, and give him such intrepidity and elevation to their character, that at times it approaches to sublimity.

JULES JANIN (1804–1874)
French critic and novelist

A woman is more responsive to a man's forgetfulness than to his attentions.

ELTON JOHN (*b.* 1947)
British rock singer
On his first love affair

At the time she was going out with a midget disc jockey – he drove a Mini with special pedals. But he used to beat her up. Then, when I lived with her, she used to beat me up. I couldn't understand it!

POPE JOHN PAUL II (*b.* 1920)

Adultery is in your heart not only when you look with excessive sexual desire at a woman who is not your wife, but also if you look in the same manner at your wife.

DR SAMUEL JOHNSON (1709–1784)
British writer
In a letter to Boswell, 19 September 1777

If I had no duties, and no references to futurity, I would spend my life in driving briskly in a post-chaise with a pretty woman.

It is as foolish to make experiments upon the constancy of a friend, as upon the chastity of a wife.

FRANKLIN P. JONES

Men seldom make passes at a girl who surpasses.

BEN JONSON (1572–1637)
British playwright
In *Celebration of Charis*

She is Venus when she smiles;
But she's Juno when she walks,
And Minerva when she talks.

JUVENAL (*c.* 55–*c.* 140)
Roman lawyer and satirist

There's no effrontery like that of a woman caught in the act: her very guilt inspires her with wrath and insolence.

HENRY KING (1592–1669)
Bishop of Chichester

And that tame Lover who unlocks his heart
Unto his mistress, teaching her an art
To plague himself, shows her the secret way
How she may tyrannize another day!

CHARLES KINGSLEY (1819–1875)
British poet
In *A Farewell to C.E.G.*

Be good, sweet maid, and let who will be clever.

In *The Three Fishers*

For men must work and women must weep,
And the sooner it's over, the sooner to sleep.

RUDYARD KIPLING (1865–1936)
British writer
In *The Female of the Species*

For the female of the species is more deadly than the male.

In *Plain Tales from the Hills*

The silliest woman can manage a clever man; but it needs a very clever woman to manage a fool.

A woman's guess is much more accurate than a man's certainty.

THE KORAN

O men, respect women who have borne you.

WALTER SAVAGE LANDOR (1775–1864)
British poet and writer

God made the rose out of what was left of woman at the creation. The great difference is, we feel the rose's thorns when we gather it, and the other's when we have had it some time.

D. H. LAWRENCE (1885–1930)
British writer
In a letter to Dr Trigant Burrow, 3 August 1927

I'm not sure if a mental relaxation with a woman doesn't make it impossible to love her. To know the *mind* of a woman is to end in hating her. Love means the precognitive flow . . . it is the honest state before the apple.

JOHN LENNON (1941–1980)
British songwriter

As usual there's a great woman behind every idiot.

ALAN J. LERNER (*b.* 1918)
British playwright and lyricist
Song lyric in *My Fair Lady*

Why can't a woman be more like a man?

JONATHAN LEVINSON Aged eight
Quoted in *New York Times*, 20 December 1974

No Girls Aloud.

C. S. LEWIS (1898–1963)
British scholar
In *The Screwtape Letters* (Preface)

Fatigue makes women talk more and men less.

She's the sort of woman who lives for others – you can always tell the others by their hunted expression.

ERIC LINKLATER (*b.* 1899)
Scottish novelist
In *Juan in America*

I've been married six months. She looks like a million dollars, but she only knows a hundred and twenty words and she's only got two ideas in her head. The other one's hats.

LIN YUTANG (1895–1976)
Chinese writer

Our ideal of womanhood in this present industrial society is that women should achieve the highest feminine attraction at the lowest cost to men.

FREDERICK LONSDALE (1881–1954)
British playwright
In *The Last of Mrs Cheyney*

To call a woman pleasant is to imply that her underwear is made of linoleum.

SAMUEL LOVER (1797–1868)
In *Handy Andy*

'Now women are mostly troublesome cattle to deal with mostly,' said Goggins.

ERNST LUBITSCH (1892–1947)
German-born Hollywood film producer

All women are sirens at heart. No matter how unemotional, how stolid, a woman may be, she has moments when her greatest desire is to be – shall we call it – a courtesan, siren or seductress. The exactly proper emotional condition and environment will bring it to the surface.

PHIL LYNOTT
Irish rock singer (*Thin Lizzy*)

Patti Smith or Olivia Newton-John . . . they're my two favourites. I could pull 'em any night.

I only became a bass player because of the girls.

GEORGE LYTTLETON (BARON LYTTLETON) (1709–1773)

Women like princes find few real friends.

COMPTON MACKENZIE (1883–1972)
British writer

Women do not find it difficult to behave like men, but they often find it difficult to behave like gentlemen.

LORD MANCROFT (*b.* 1914)
British politician

If [your wife] happens to be travelling anywhere without

you and you want her back in a hurry, send her a copy of your local newspaper with a little paragraph cut out.

DON MARQUIS (1878–1937)
American writer

The females of all species are most dangerous when they appear to retreat.

ANDREW MARVELL (1620–1678)
British poet
In *To His Coy Mistress*

Had we but world enough, and time,
This coyness, lady, were no crime.

GROUCHO MARX (1895–1977)
American comedian

Mistresses are more common in California – in fact some of them are very common. It's easier for a man to conceal his mistress there because of the smog.

She got her good looks from her father – he's a plastic surgeon.

Behind every great man is a woman. And behind her is his wife.

To a Hollywood hostess

I've had a wonderful evening – but this wasn't it.

JACKIE MASON

Today when a woman says 'I do', that's the last thing she does.

WILLIAM H. MASTERS
American sexologist

Males have made asses of themselves writing about the female sexual experience.

W. SOMERSET MAUGHAM (1874–1965)
British writer
In *The Moon and Sixpence*

A woman can forgive a man for the harm he does her, but she can never forgive him for the sacrifices he makes on her account.

ANDRÉ MAUROIS (1885–1967)
French writer
In *Ariel*

Housekeeping in common is for women the acid test.

FRANK MCKINNEY

The rich man and his daughter are soon parted.

H. L. MENCKEN (1880–1956)
American critic
In *In Defense of Women*

It takes no more actual sagacity to carry on the everyday hawking and haggling of the world, or to ladle out its normal doses of bad medicine and worse law, than it takes to operate a taxicab or fry a pan of fish.

A man's womenfolk, whatever their outward show of respect for his merit and authority, always regard him secretly as an ass, and with something akin to pity.

I can't remember a single masculine figure created by a woman who is not, at bottom, a booby.

In *The Incomparable Buzz-Saw*

The allurement that women hold out to men is precisely the allurement that Cape Hatteras holds out to sailors: they are enormously dangerous and hence enormously fascinating.

In *Prejudices* (4th Series)

Women hate revolutions and revolutionists. They like men who are docile, and well-regarded at the bank, and never late at meals.

GEORGE MEREDITH (1842–1913)
British poet
In *Love in the Valley*

She whom I love is harder to catch and conquer,
Hard, but O the glory of the winning were she won!

Woman's reason is in the milk of her breasts.

JOHN STUART MILL (1806–1893)
British philosopher

One can, to an almost laughable degree, infer what a man's wife is like from his opinions about women in general.

OLIN MILLER

A man who won't lie to a woman has very little consideration for her feelings.

A. A. MILNE (1882–1956)
British writer
In *Going Out to Dinner*

It is only the very young girl at her first dinner party whom it is difficult to entertain. At her second dinner party and thereafter, she knows the whole art of being amusing. All she has to do is to listen; all we men have to do is tell her about ourselves.

THOMAS MOORE (1779–1852)
British poet

My only books
Were woman's looks,
And folly's all they've taught me.

Disguise our bondage as we will,
'Tis woman, woman, rules us still.

J. B. MORTON ('Beachcomber') (1883–1979)
British humorist

She has a Rolls body and a Balham mind.

RALPH NADER (*b.* 1934)
American consumer campaigner

Young wives are the leading asset of corporate power. They want the suburbs, a house, a settled life. And respectability. They want society to see that they have exchanged themselves for something of value.

OGDEN NASH (1902–1971)
American poet

I hope my tongue in prune juice smothers
If I belittle dogs and mothers.

LORD NELSON (1758–1805)
English admiral

Brave Emma – Good Emma – If there were more Emmas there would be more Nelsons.

FRIEDRICH WILHELM NIETZSCHE (1844–1900)
German philosopher

A woman may very well form a friendship with a man, but for this to endure, it must be assisted by a little physical antipathy.

Women themselves always still have in the background of all personal vanity an impersonal contempt for 'woman'.

Woman's vanity demands that a man be more than a happy husband.

Woman understands children better than man does, but man is more childlike than woman.

DENIS NORDEN (*b.* 1922)
British humorist

It's a funny kind of month, October. For the really keen cricket fan it's when you discover that your wife left you in May.

BARRY NORMAN (*b.* 1933)
British critic

Perhaps at fourteen every boy should be in love with some ideal woman to put on a pedestal and worship. As he grows up, of course, he will put her on a pedestal the better to view her legs.

ARISTOTLE ONASSIS (1906–1975)
Greek shipping tycoon

If women didn't exist, all the money in the world would have no meaning.

JOE ORTON (1933–1967)
British playwright

Women are like banks, boy. Breaking and entering is a serious business.

THOMAS OTWAY (1652–1685)
English dramatist
In *Venice Preserved*

Oh woman! lovely woman! Nature made thee
To temper man: we had been brutes without you;
Angels are painted fair, to look like you;
There's in you all that we believe of heav'n,
Amazing brightness, purity, and truth,
Eternal joy, and everlasting love.

In *The Orphan*

Destructive, damnable, deceitful woman!

OVID (43 BC–AD 18)
Latin poet
In *The Art of Love*

I could not possibly count the gold-digging ruses of women,
Not if I had ten mouths, not if I had ten tongues.

MOHAMMED REZA PAHLEVI (1919–1980)
Shah of Iran

Women when they are in power are much harsher than men.

Much more cruel. Much more bloodthirsty. I'm quoting facts, not opinions.

PANCHANTANTRA (*c.* 5th century)

Kings, women, and creeping vines as a rule embrace whatever is beside them.

CESARE PAVESE (1908–1950)
Italian novelist

Woman gives herself as a prize to the weak and a prop to the strong, and no man ever has what he should.

THOMAS LOVE PEACOCK (1785–1866)
British novelist
In *Nightmare Abbey*

Sir, I have quarrelled with my wife; and a man who has quarrelled with his wife is absolved from all duty to his country.

SAMUEL PEPYS (1633–1703)
English diarist

Music and women I cannot but give way to, whatever my business is.

THOMAS PERCY (1728–1811)
English poet
In *The Friar of Orders Gray*

Sigh no more, ladies, sigh no more!
Men were deceivers ever;
One foot in sea and one on shore,
To one thing constant never.

LAURENCE J. PETER (*b.* 1919)
Canadian educator

She has as much originality as a Xerox machine.

DR H. R. PICKARD
'Sayings of the Week' (*Observer*, 7 October 1928)

If you give a girl an inch nowadays she will make a dress of it.

SIR ARTHUR WING PINERO (1955–1934)
British playwright

Regret is a woman's natural food – she thrives upon it.

LUIGI PIRANDELLO (1867–1936)
Italian dramatist

Women are like dreams – they are never the way you would like to have them.

PLAUTUS (250–184 BC)
Roman playwright

Women have too many faults, but the worst of them all is that they are too pleased with themselves and take too little pains to please the men.

ALEXANDER POPE (1688–1744)
British poet

Women, as they are like riddles in being unintelligible, so generally resemble them in this, that they please us no longer once we know them.

Woman's at best a contradiction still.

STEPHEN POTTER (1900–1969)
British writer

Women are quite unlike men. Women have higher voices, longer hair, smaller waistlines, daintier feet and prettier hands. They also invariably have the upper hand.

MATTHEW PRIOR (1664–1721)
English poet

Be to her virtues very kind;
Be to her faults a little blind.

WILLIAM PRYNNE (1600–1669)
English puritan pamphleteer

The dissolutenesse of our lascivious, impudent, rattle-pated gadding females now is such . . . they are lowde and stubborne; their feet abide not in their houses; now they are without, now in the streets, and lie in wait at every corner, being never well pleased nor contented but when they are wandering abroad to Playes, to Playhouses, Dancing-Matches, Masques, and publicke Shewes.

JEAN PAUL RICHTER (1762–1825)
German novelist

Women do not properly understand that when an idea fills and elevates a man's mind it shuts out love and crowds out people.

VICTOR RIESEL

Frailty, thy name is no longer woman.

WILL ROGERS (1879–1935)
American humorist

The whole thing about the woman is, they lust to be misunderstood.

GIOACCHINO ROSSINI (1792–1868)
Italian composer

I have all the women's ills. All I lack is the uterus.

PHILIP ROTH (*b.* 1933)
American novelist

It's the little questions from women about tappets that finally push men over the edge.

ARTUR RUBINSTEIN (1888–1982)
American pianist

It is said of me that when I was young, I divided my time impartially among wine, women, and song. I deny this categorically. Ninety per cent of my interests were women.

When I was young, I used to have successes with women because I was young. Now I have successes with women because I am old. Middle age was the hardest part.

DAMON RUNYON (1884–1946)
American author and humorist

Even Mr Justin Veezee is not so old-fashioned as to believe any doll will go to his apartment just to look at etchings nowadays.

If I am interested in the kissing and hugging business, I will most certainly take my business to Marie, especially as she speaks English, and you will not have to waste time with the sign language.

Charlotte is not such a doll as cares to spend more than one or two years looking at the pictures on the wall.

BERTRAND RUSSELL (1872–1970)
British philosopher

Male domination has had some very unfortunate effects. It has made the most intimate of human relations, that of marriage, one of master and slave, instead of one between equal partners.

SAKI (H. H. MUNRO) (1870–1916)
British novelist
In *The Unbearable Bassington*

To see her standing at the top of an expensively horticultured staircase receiving her husband's guests was rather like watching an animal performing on a music-hall stage. One always tells oneself that the animal likes it, and one always knows that it doesn't.

The woman who can sacrifice a clean unspoiled penny stamp is probably unborn.

In *The Watched Pot*

Woman is a belated survival from a primeval age of struggle and competition; that is why, the world over, you find all the superfluous dust and worry being made by the gentler sex.

CARLOS SANTANA (*b.* 1947)
American rock performer

I know that when I leave my hair longer I start attracting certain vibrations from certain ladies that I really don't need. I started looking in the mirror too much.

JEAN-PAUL SARTRE (1905–1980)
French philosopher

She believed in nothing; only her scepticism kept her from being an atheist.

RONALD SEARLE (*b.* 1920)
British artist

In the spring . . . your lovely Chloe lightly turns to one mass of spots.

GEORGE SEATON
In *The Country Girl*, screenplay for Paramount, 1954

There are two kinds of women – those who pay too much attention to themselves and those who don't pay enough.

MACK SENNETT (1880–1960)
American film maker

We never make sport of religion, politics, race, or mothers. A mother never gets hit with a custard pie. Mothers-in-law – yes. But mothers – never.

PETER SHAFFER (*b.* 1926)
British playwright
In *Equus*

All my wife has ever taken from the Mediterranean – from that whole vast intuitive culture – are four bottles of Chianti to make into lamps, and two china condiment donkeys labelled Sally and Peppy.

WILLIAM SHAKESPEARE (1564–1616)
English playwright
In *The Comedy of Errors*

The pleasing punishment that women bear.

In *Hamlet*

Frailty, thy name is woman!

In *King Lear*

There was never yet fair woman but she made mouths in a glass.

Her voice was ever soft,
Gentle and low, an excellent thing in woman.

In *Love's Labour's Lost*

A child of our grandmother Eve, a female; or, for thy more sweet understanding, a woman.

From women's eyes this doctrine I derive:
They sparkle still the right Promethean fire;
They are the books, the arts, the academes,
That show, contain, and nourish all the world.

In *Othello*

She never yet was foolish that was fair.

In *Romeo and Juliet*

A woman moved is like a fountain troubled,
Muddy, ill-seeming, thick, bereft of beauty.

In *As You Like It*

Do you not know I am a woman? When I think, I must speak.

OMAR SHARIF (*b.* 1932)
Egyptian-born actor

The trouble with women in love is that they are too generous; give too much. Men don't really like this. On the other hand, if a woman is offhand they don't like that either. There is no answer.

Quoted in *The Times*, 11 July 1983

I really am a mother's boy. I adore her and she adores me. She's not just proud of me – she faints when she sees me. She gets hysterical. If she were here now she'd want me to sit on her knee.

GEORGE BERNARD SHAW (1856–1950)
Irish playwright
In *Candida*

A man ought to be able to be fond of his wife without making a fool of himself about her.

In *Man and Superman*

It is a woman's business to get married as soon as possible, and a man's to keep unmarried as long as he can.

Home is the girl's prison and the woman's workhouse.

Marry Ann and at the end of the week you'll find no more inspiration in her than in a plate of muffins.

Vitality in a woman is a blind fury of creation.

She'll commit every crime a respectable woman can; and she'll justify every one of them by saying that it was the wish of her guardians.

In *Pygmalion*

Women upset everything. When you let them into your life, you find that the woman is driving at one thing and you're driving at another.

In a letter to Alice Lockett

Lovemaking grows tedious to me – the emotion has evaporated from it. This is your fault.

RICHARD BRINSLEY SHERIDAN (1751–1816)
Irish-born playwright
To an unnamed young lady

Won't you come into the garden? I would like my roses to see you.

In *The Critic*

O Lord, sir, when a heroine goes mad she always goes into white satin.

SIR OSBERT SITWELL (1892–1969)
British poet and novelist
In *Great Morning*

She belonged to the superannuated dairy-maid type, and possessed a voice that, like a mill, ground silence into its component parts.

ALEXANDER SOLZHENITSYN (*b.* 1918)
Russian novelist
In a letter to Soviet leaders

We are always boasting about our equality for women and our kindergartens but we hide the fact that all this is just a substitute for the family we have undermined. Equality for women doesn't mean that they have to occupy *the same number* of factory jobs and office positions as men, but just that all these posts should in principle be equally open to women.

SPANISH PROVERB

The nightingale will run out of songs before a woman runs out of conversation.

DR BENJAMIN SPOCK (*b.* 1903)
American paediatrician

Women are usually more patient in working at unexciting repetitive tasks.

RICHARD STEELE (1671–1729)
English essayist

These ladies of irresistible modesty are those who make virtue unamiable.

A woman seldom writes her mind but in her postscript.

EDWARD STEICHEN
American photographer

Women – the greatest undeveloped natural resource in the world today.

HENRI BEYLE DE STENDHAL (1783–1842)
French writer

Such is the rule of modesty, a woman of feeling betrays her sentiments for her lover sooner by deed than by word.

A wise woman never yields by appointment.

Women are always eagerly on the lookout for any emotion.

ROBERT SMITH SURTEES (1803–1864)
British writer
In *Mr Sponge's Sporting Tour*

Women never look so well as when one comes in wet and dirty from hunting.

The young ladies entered the drawing-room in the full fervour of sisterly animosity.

In *Mr Facey Romford's Hounds*

The real business of a ball is either to look out for a wife, to look after a wife, or to look after somebody else's wife.

ITALO SVEVO (1861–1928)
Italian novelist

The really original woman is the one who first imitates a man.

TAKI (Takis Theodorakis)
Greek-born gossip columnist

It is a mark of civilized men that they defend their women.

TALLEYRAND (Charles Maurice de Périgord-Talleyrand) (1754–1838)
French statesman

Women sometimes forgive those who force an opportunity, never those who miss it.

ALFRED, LORD TENNYSON (1809–1892)
British poet
In *Edwin Morris*

God made the woman for the man,
And for the good and increase of the world.

In *The Princess*

Man is the hunter; woman is his game
The sleek and shining creatures of the chase,
We hunt them for the beauty of their skins.

The woman is so hard
Upon the woman.

WILLIAM MAKEPEACE THACKERAY (1811–1863)
British novelist
In *Mr Brown's Letters*

When I say that I know women, I mean I know that I don't know them. Every single woman I ever knew is a puzzle to me, as, I have no doubt, she is to herself.

In *Esmond*

'Tis strange what a man may do, and a woman yet think him an angel.

In *Lovel the Widower*

What woman, however old, has not the bridal favours and raiment stowed away, and packed in lavender, in the inmost cupboards of her heart?

In *Vanity Fair*

I think I could be a good woman if I had five thousand a year (Becky Sharp).

JAMES THURBER (1894–1961)
American humorist

She said he proposed something on their wedding night her own brother wouldn't have suggested.

LEO TOLSTOY (1828–1910)
Russian writer

When I have one foot in the grave I will tell the truth about women. I shall tell it, jump into my coffin, pull the lid over me and say, 'Do what you like now.'

In *Anna Karenina*

There is trouble with a wife, but it's even worse with a woman who is not a wife.

CYRIL TOURNEUR (1575–1626)
British playwright
In *The Revenger's Tragedy*

Were't not for gold and women, there would be no damnation.

PIERRE TRUDEAU (*b.* 1919)
Canadian Prime Minister

I do not like indiscreet women.

FRANCOIS TRUFFAUT (*b.* 1932)
French film director

Being a woman is a profession whose only patron is God.

MARK TWAIN (Samuel Langhorne Clemens) (1835–1910)
American novelist

A woman springs a sudden reproach upon you which provokes a hot retort – and then she will presently ask you to apologize.

She was not quite what you would call refined. She was not quite what you would call unrefined. She was the kind of person that keeps a parrot.

KENNETH TYNAN (1927–1980)
British critic

A century and a half ago there were no knickers and girls read the Bible, now they wear impenetrable body stockings and read *Portnoy's Complaint*.

RICHARD USBORNE (*b.* 1910)
British critic
In *Wodehouse at Work to the End*

A monstrous aunt can be funny. A monstrous mother would be tragic.

SIR JOHN VANBRUGH (1664–1726)
English playwright
In *The Confederacy*

As if a woman of education bought things because she wanted 'em.

In *The Relapse*

No man worth having is true to his wife, or can be true to his wife, or ever was, or ever will be so.

VIRGIL (70–19 BC)
Roman poet

Woman is always fickle and changing.

W. R. WALLACE (1873–1966)
British politician
In *John o' London's Treasure Trove*

The hand that rocks the cradle
Is the hand that rules the world.

ARTEMUS WARD (Charles Farrar Brown) (1834–1867)
American humorist

The female woman is one of the greatest institooshuns of which this land can boste.

CHARLES DUDLEY WARNER (1829–1900)
American writer

There is nothing that disgusts a man like getting beaten at chess by a woman.

Woman is perpetual revolution, and is that element in the world which continually destroys and re-creates.

EVELYN WAUGH (1903–1966)
British novelist
In *Scoop*

'I will not stand for being called a woman in my own house,' she said.

JOHN WEITZ

When a woman dresses up for an occasion, the man should become the black velvet pillow for the jewel.

ORSON WELLES (*b.* 1915)
American actor

The basic and essential human is the woman.

If there hadn't been women we'd still be squatting in a cave eating raw meat, because we made civilization in order to impress our girlfriends.

H. G. WELLS (1866–1946)
British novelist and sociologist
In *Select Conversations with an Uncle*

I sometimes think that if Adam and Eve had been merely engaged, she would not have talked with the serpent; and the world had been saved an infinity of misery.

In *Kipps*

'It's giving girls names like that [Euphemia],' said Buggins, 'that nine times out of ten makes 'em go wrong. It unsettles 'em. If ever I was to have a girl, if ever I was to have a dozen girls, I'd call 'em all Jane.'

E. B. WHITE (*b.* 1899)
American essayist

The dream of the American male is for a female who has an essential languor which is not laziness, who is unaccompanied except by himself, and who does not let him down. He desires a beautiful, but comprehensible creature who does not destroy a perfect situation by forming a complete sentence.

OSCAR WILDE (1854–1900)
Irish writer
In *A Woman of No Importance*

Nothing spoils a romance so much as a sense of humour in the woman.

In *The Importance of Being Earnest*

All women become like their mothers. That is their tragedy. No man does. That's his.

In *Lady Windermere's Fan*

There is nothing in the whole world so unbecoming to a woman as a nonconformist conscience.

In *The Picture of Dorian Gray*

Women represent the triumph of matter over mind, just as men represent the triumph of mind over morals.

Women are a decorative sex. They never have anything to say, but they say it charmingly.

On an American hostess of the 1890s

Poor woman, she tried to open a salon, but only succeeded in opening a saloon.

TENNESSEE WILLIAMS (1911–1983)
American playwright
In *The Night of the Iguana*

Hysteria is a natural phenomenon, the common denominator of the female nature. It's the big female weapon, and the test of a man is his ability to cope with it.

EARL WILSON (*b.* 1907)
American journalist

A woman may race to get a man a gift but it always ends in a tie.

SLOAN WILSON (*b.* 1920)
American novelist

The definition of a beautiful woman is one who loves me.

GEORGE WITHER (1588–1667)
English poet
In *The Author's Resolution*

Shall I, wasting in despair,
Die because a woman's fair?
Or make pale my cheeks with care,
'Cause another's rosy are?
Be she fairer than the day,
Or the flowery meads in May,
  If she be not so to me,
  What care I how fair she be?

SIR HENRY WOTTON (1568–1639)
English scholar
In *A Woman's Heart*

Love lodged in a woman's breast
Is but a guest.

WILLIAM WYCHERLEY (*c.* 1640–1716)
British playwright
In *The Plain Dealer*

A man no more believes a woman when she says she has an aversion for him than when she says she'll cry out.

Well, a widow, I see, is a kind of sinecure.

W. B. YEATS (1865–1939)
Irish poet
On Lady Gregory

She has been a mother, friend, sister and brother. I cannot realize the world without her – she brought to my wavering thoughts steadfast nobility. All day the thought of losing her is like a conflagration in the rafters. Friendship is all the house I have.

JOSÉ YGLESIAS (*b.* 1945)
Spanish singer

Women make much better soldiers than men. They always know where the real enemy is hidden.